Allison the Mail Order Bride An Anthology of Frontier & Amish Romance

Victoria Morton

Published by Trellis Publishing, 2021.

This is a work of fiction. Similarities to real people, places, or events are entirely coincidental.

ALLISON THE MAIL ORDER BRIDE AN ANTHOLOGY OF FRONTIER & AMISH ROMANCE

First edition. June 28, 2021.

Copyright © 2021 Victoria Morton.

ISBN: 979-8224327836

Written by Victoria Morton.

ALLISON THE MAIL ORDER BRIDE

VICTORIA MORTON

The wastelands were said to be dangerous at night and she knew it but she knew she had to cross it to get the tavern at the other side of town. She had visited the tavern while she was a little girl in the past with her dad. Allison adjusted her cowgirl hat and geared the horse towards the east. The inn had been converted to a motel as its ownership had swapped hands. Luckily for her, it still had a make shift stall where she could leave her horse at least for the night. She had no money left on her. She practically had nothing. Her former employer had blackmailed her and forced her into the streets and her brother had settled for melting metals and shaping them into tools somewhere in Ontario. He had suggested she offered to take out mugs bearing alcohol stinks and that of the men drinking from them at the Inn. She had barely poked her head through the doors when she discovered that wasn't the type of life she wanted. Being a bar attendant wasn't her thing, she only realized that later while she picked herself off the floor of the streets after having been thrown out for giving one of the many visitors a knee jab to the groins after he had grabbed her ass. She needed something better than that. Something that reels in more bucks than strutting about with a corset that was hell bent on snuffing life out of her. Her parents' death had thought her to be tough these few years. She had wandered the wastelands hoping for her sake she didn't run into any bounty hunters. They had a thing for females especially ones that looked fragile and defenseless. She was a little bit of both as she knew she stood defenseless if she were to run into any of the famous bounty hunters. Her boldness was just a front to keep men at bay. She was soft at heart but that wasn't her problem at the moment.

Looking up at lights that illuminated the name of the Motel, she stepped into the frigid warmth of the reception.

"The place is booked for the day now if you wouldn't mind finding some other place to settle in for the night," the elderly man behind the reception desk said as he adjusted his spectacles.

"I've come a long way if you'd please pity my poor legs and eyes that need some rest. You could fix me up somewhere," Allison said batting her eyes as she removed her hat letting her hair fall to its full length, her charm had never failed her and she could see the effect of her charm as the man scratched his stubble and sized her up. *She'd be good for business if only she'd agree to it*, he thought.

"And what would you pay me with, that diamond ring of yours would fetch a handsome pay. What do you say? He said eyeing her left middle finger with a flickering grin. She had studied the guy. He could fall prey of any mischief if the bait was a woman – a beautiful young woman. Allison was all that, young, beautiful and full of life and he was gullible too. So she decided to prey on the former factor.

"That was mum's and she handed it to me right before she died, I couldn't trade that for oxygen itself but I'll be willing to give up my horse. I wouldn't be needing it anyway as I have no other place in mind to stay after here.

"Alright, while you are here make yourself at home and feel free to call me up if you need services in other departments," he said with a cunning smile playing at the corners of his mouth. Allison's eyes darted to the daily post on the wall behind him and her eyes caught on the post with a bold inscription saying "PRETTY LADIES WANTED FOR ORDER." She needed money but at that moment, a beautiful sleep would have been the best gift ever. So taking the key from him and swiping her hat off the desk she walked off to her room.

The musky scent of the room welcomed her with open arms. She knew that scent belonged to a woman and there was this other scent, it tasted masculine to the hairs in her nostrils. She tugged at her itchy tight pants and when she had her clothing lying few feet away from her, she plopped on the bed and making a mental note to attend to her money issues later, she let her tired eyes the liberty to rest.

***

Bradley struggled to keep up with the powerful strides of sleep but little Alonzo wouldn't let him. He had been woken up by the terrifying sound of the thunder bolt.

"C'mon Alonzo, some sleep will be appreciated you know," Bradley muttered with frustration as he made his way to the next room immediately after his. Alonzo was his late twin sister's son who was fortunate to have survived the C-section that let him into the world. His father abandoned his sister Emile when he got wave she was pregnant with his child and since that day his embittered self had sworn to kill him if he ever set his eyes on him. He initiated his sister's death anyway and so doesn't deserve the privilege of roaming the earth while she was somewhere below the earth. He held him to his chest cupping his butt firmly patted his back gently to put him back to sleep. He hadn't any experiences with kids, this was his first and he was pretty proud of himself for having nursed the 2 year old who cried of his momma always. He needed to get someone to take care of him. A female figure who knew a lot about babies, what was he saying all females should know how to handle babies. It's their specialty, he thought. Someone he wouldn't have to pay to do the job. Since Emile's demise, he found out that he was lonely and it was only a woman's colorful touch that could fix his loneliness. He wasn't sure how to go about handling that factor as his past relationships barely got past a week. Women in that part of Bunbury were scared of him as he was the hostile sort. He was a man of his own thoughts and so you dared not interfere with yours. The one woman he had ever loved with all sincerity was his sister. He's old man was dead now and he never got to know his mother as he died few months after his birth. He cared not about other people's opinion and so couldn't stay in any relationship as he couldn't handle a female trying to share her opinion with him in the name of love. That to him was major bullcrap. He had once beaten up a girlfriend of his for redesigning his closet. He was a man of his own and so would feel like a second to no one. He expected whoever he would court or marry to respect his wishes and do whatever she was told to do whether or not she enjoyed doing it. His love was just for his sister and Alonzo. Alonzo who seemed to hear his thoughts shifted in his arms and nestled his head close to his neck. Bradley smiled at that cute search by the little boy for comfort. He had a soft spot for him and would always will. That wasn't a surprise as he was his own blood and from his twin. He walked back to his room with little Alonzo in his arms. The only way he was going to get a good night's rest was if Alonzo could get one too and he wasn't going to if he wasn't snuggled close to warmth. Even the little boy got lonely sometimes and understood the importance of that body heat that emanated from the skin.

"Hello who's in here," Carter called from the patio. He sat on one of the seats and lit his pipe. Bradley stirred when he heard his friend's voice. He laid still when Alonzo stirred in his sleep. Gradually he slipped out of his bed making sure not to disturb the sleeping Alonzo. He knew who it was that could walk in that early to disrupt his sleep and he was glad he always did. He was one person he could always talk to. Carter was the true friend he had from the factory; the others were there because he was the manager of the place and so have to be loyal in order to be on his good side. He had been friends with Carter since his childhood so it was no surprise they worked in the same place and still had ties to each other.

"Hey bud. Up early today huh?" he said and walked up to the patio to shake and hug Carter.

"Baby sitting again?" carter asked trying to stifle his yawn. Man you should get a babysitter of some sort or you could actually get married. Have your lady take care of him."

"Get married? What for?

"For Alonzo," Carter replied curtly. Bradley signaled his butler to get them drinks. The old man had just stepped in to begin his work for the day and so hurried into the house when he saw his boss's signal.

"I don't get what you are trying to say. That I can't take care of Alonzo?" Bradley asked with raised eyebrows.

"I am saying you should get a woman to take care of Alonzo and to take care of your bed room needs man. I practically am awed to know that you have survived this long without a woman's touch. What are you a monk?"

"Oh come off it Carter, I can handle Alonzo. I've been a great dad these past months to him, so give me some credit I'm doing better than I had thought I would. And the ladies here wouldn't even get near me due to my principled nature. I doubt any woman would be able to handle me."

"Principled nature huh? Well this debate is for another day, for now you can't go drinking and diving with me because of him. I'm afraid he would even gradually turn you into a woman pretty soon, all soft hearted and clingy."

Bradley threw his head back and laughed. You know that's not possible. Bradley secretly craved a woman who would understand why he was that way. If only they can understand that I have always been like this because of my roots and the fact I've grown to always be in charge," he sighed. He watched as his butler poured them wine. He stared at the glass for some time lost in thoughts. His friend was right; he needed to get back to the factory, to hanging out with his buddy. He couldn't do that with Alonzo hanging from his neck. Carter who figured out midway into his next sentence that his friend had zoned him out waved his hands before his eyes to snap him out from whatever island he had strayed into.

"Hey, stay with me man. What's with the worry lines? Are you beginning to realize the truth behind the fact that I just stated?"

"It's not been easy and won't be. The females here hate me," Bradley said sighing with exasperation.

"They don't. They just don't want to have anything to do with you," Carter retorted lowering his glass to the table before him.

"That's just about the same thing I'm saying here."

"Well, you can forget about the ladies here and go for the ones in other faraway countries that don't know about you. Women who are willing to come over to Australia once you are ready to process their passport."

"I'm not about to get a whore to take care of my child, no I'm not," Bradley said with a note of finality in his voice and gulped down what was left of his wine.

"And who's talking of having Alonzo grow under the care of a whore? I'm talking of a mail order bride Brad," Carter said leaning forward on the table and studying his friend's reactions. He hadn't thought it would result to this but this was the only shot he had to get back to his life which he had left for some months now to take care of Alonzo.

"Does that still exist?"

"Yeah, it does for confused bachelors like you. Or should I say principled bachelors," he teased and broke off into laughter. When he looked up and saw Bradley was in no laughing mood he gradually ceased his laughter. "I'm sorry man but I have to point out the obvious," he said holding his stomach to calm his laughing self. "The factory needs your presence I can't handle things there alone anymore. I need my bud back. You can have it both ways if you have a woman by your side to take care of you and Alonzo. You should give that thought a lot of considerations."

"Fine, I'll think about that. Now can you stop making fun of my situation and stop laughing so hard or you'll wake him," Brad said with a frown.

"If I don't tease you, who will? James maybe?" He said as his words threw him into another fit of laughter. James was the name of his butler.

"C'mon man, Alonzo," Brad cautioned in a hushed tone.

"Fine," Carter said hands in the air in mock surrender. "I decided to stop by on my way to the factory to see how my young mother was doing, he teased again. Brad was used to his frequent teasing so he just went with the flow and attempted a twirl to show off his bulging muscles and fine abs.

"What do you think?" he said with a fake grin.

"Perfect," Carter laughed and suddenly they heard Alonzo's cries from the building.

"Okay now that's my cue," carter picked up his keys and headed out towards his car. "See you later mate and by the way I heard Italian mail order brides make great wives," he said giving Brad a mock salute before hurrying off to his car which was parked in Brad's garage.

A sad smiled crawled past Brad's lips. He missed the factory and working alongside Carter. Tackling business partners and meetings with his sidekick was one of the best moments in his life. A sudden craving to get back to his life washed over him and he walked into the house to attend to Alonzo's needs. He really needed to get back to being himself even if he needed the help of a mail order bride for that to happen.

***

Allison woke up to the sound of birds chirping and animal calls to each other. She didn't expect less as the motel was at the outskirts of an Italian town in the west and her room had a nice view of the town. She walked into the bathroom to have her first bath in what seemed like ages. Her room had a decent tub and the hot water tap still functioned and so blocking the drainage with a piece of cloth she could find, she ran herself a warm bath. She stepped into the tub of warm soapy water and stretched in her full length as she let the water seep into her pores and caress her tired skin. She scrubbed until she was sure she had gotten rid of the dirt her body had accumulated from the long journey to Portofino. That was the name of the town. She had seen it on her way into the town. Her stomach growled reminding her that she hadn't had anything to eat since she got into town. She decided to tour the town to know if she could find someone hiring. She had no money and ha o horses to trade anymore. She hopped for someone who might be willing to help a stranger with some food. She walked down the rickety stairs that were hanging onto rusty nails.

"Hey pretty, you up already? Come to thank me for the nice room and possibly the hot tub?"

"Yeah sure thanks for that. Know of any good place I could get a decent meal?" Allison asked leaning on the reception desk.

"Yeah sure, there's a café around the corner. They make really nice beef jerky and burger," he said as he tore his eyes away from her and continued clicking on his laptop.

"Thanks." Allison said and stood to leave when her eyes went to the wall and the poster from the day before caught her attention for the second time stopping her in her tracks.

"What is that all about?" She asked pointing at the poster. That's some business of mine, you interested to sign up for ordering?

"Order, what crap are you talking about? You think I'm some merchandise now?" she asked standing on the defensive.

"Mail order brides are literally merchandise meant to be ordered by men who resort to marrying wives from the set displayed on our catalogue. You could accumulate some handsome money just being a mail order bride and did I forget? That bride is entitled to a passport to whatever country her online groom orders her from. And I heard you mention something about wanting a passport in your sleep," he said with a coy smile.

"In my sleep? You were peeking on me?" She shouted all of a sudden realizing he must have seen her bath too.

"No. No. you dialed the reception this morning asking for a hot bath. So I assumed you called because you noticed the heater linked to your bathroom was off, so I went to put it on.

"I called you? This morning?" she asked sounding surprised? "What time was that?"

He scrolled up the customer's call log and checked for Room 206. "That should be around 7.30AM. I was surprised you were up that early. You sounded groggy though."

She checked her time and it was 10AM already. "I don't remember calling you, must have called while I was still sleepy. I guess I slept of right after the call," she said still looking confused.

"Maybe," he shrugged and continued clicking without throwing her another glance.

"Oh well the offer on the wall is quite tempting but I'll pass. I'd like to get a genuine job around though but being married off to some guy I don't know isn't my idea of a good job."

"The town is a welcoming one. Knock yourself out. I doubt you will be successful on the aspect of the job hunt anyway. Now if you wouldn't mind hand me the keys to the room and you can be on your merry way," he said stretching out his left hand and beckoning for the keys.

"Here you go," she said tossing him the keys which he caught in the air.

"Nice catch," she said with a smile and stepped out into the street.

Portofino had an even beautiful view from where she stood. The streets were busy with carts being drawn by horses. They seemed to be making their way to and fro a milk factory as they were stacked with cartons of milk to be sold. She tore her eyes off the horses in search of the Cafe the receptionist had mentioned when her stomach reminded her of how hungry she was. She clutched her stomach as of to hush it.

"You behave alright, I'll soon get you something to chew on," she said as she veered off the street into the corner she thought the Cafe would be on. Few strides into the street she spotted a Cafe and walking into it inquired if they were hiring but she was met with a negative reply.

She walked about town for some time and every place she went to, met her at the door with a negative reply.

Later on towards evening she walked into the motel tired out. She had been able to eat at the Cafe after having washed most of the plates.

The receptionist watched her enter the Motel and plop onto one of the settees in the lobby.

"Any luck with the job hunt?" Allison who was tired out from the fruitless job hunt shook her head in negation.

"You are pretty enough for a typical Mail order bride. You should consider it." he said and paused to know if he would get any reaction from her that say she was game. When he saw she was beginning to pay heed to what he was sayin, he decided to bait her.

"Fine, I'll make a deal with you.You can decide to withdraw if you don't like your husband and I'll pay him whatever amount he paid for your order without collecting anything from you. I just need one more bride aboard. You need this Ms. Allison he said hoping his speech would change her mind. And it did. She was in desperate need of a way out of her dilemma. Before long she had subscribed to his idea and now the waiting began. She had the idea of the perfect husband in her head but she had to condition her mind to accept whoever would order her. "This is just for the meantime, it sure isn't forever," she said to console herself as she walked back to her room.

***

Alonzo's cries sent Bradley flying to his room the second time for the night. He cursed under his breath when his yells cut through the silent veils of the night yet again. His voice had grown strong and his cries could wake the dead if he was ever brought close to a cemetery. Bradley had just noticed his cries came whenever his back kissed the mattress in his cot.

"Oh C'mon Alonzo, you have to understand that Daddy has got work first thing tomorrow morning... I'm going back to work after my long holiday. He was gradually getting frustrated and he knew it wasn't Alonzo's fault and so he couldn't take it out on him. He was just a child what did he know anyway, he thought as a sigh escaped his lips. Holding little Alonzo so that his head was resting on his shoulder he walked towards his laptop and once it was booted typed Mail order bride in his browser. A site popped open when he clicked on Italian mail order brides.

He scrolled through the pictures that popped up and stopped immediately he caught a glimpse of her. She was beautiful and looked just right for the job he needed done. Her clipped bio read;

Allison Jenkins

24years

Loves babysitting

He clicked on order and sealed the deal with the payments he made online for her travels. She would be arriving in two days' time. He hoped he'd be able to cope in these two days. He loved Alonzo but he couldn't handle him alone, Carter was right. He needed help and Allison would soon be there to rescue him. He smiled as he drifted off to sleep with Alonzo lying on his chest.

***

"Ma'am, you've gotta see this," the receptionist rushed towards Allison as she made her way down the stairs to begin the days hustle for jobs. He half-dragged and half-walked her towards his desk.

"What is that Bonfilio?" She asked. She had overheard his name the other day while he was speaking to some new client of his on the phone.

"You've been ordered Ma'am, he said grinning from cheek to cheek. You have until next tomorrow to get ready. You're leaving in two days' time.

"That was really sudden, Allison exclaimed not sure she was thrilled about being a wife to someone he knew nothing about.

"How do I get to locate him? Did he say anything about where he lives?"

"Nah nothing, you will just look out for your name on the placard in the crowd when you land at the airport. Someone will be there to get you." He sounded confident and reassuring and so she decided to trust that. It was all she could hold on to.

The next day Bonfilio took her to a spa to get her looking like a bride and got her ladies dresses to go with her new look. She was glad to be out of her grimy leather suit and boots.

The next day Allison touched down Bunbury, Australia and just like she had been instructed began to look for her name in crowd waiting to pick up a friend or family member. She saw a guy with a placard with her name on it.He was practically glued to his phone and so didn't notice her until she came up to him and tapped him.

"Oh, hey there. To what do I owe the pleasure of being accosted by a princess?" Carter who had opted to help pick up Bradley pick up his bride said glancing past her and around to see if a lady was looking stranded anywhere around him.

"I'm Allison."

"Oh really, that's beautiful. Can I call you Al?"

"Sure. Knock yourself out."

She is good and sexy, he thought as he smiled. "Brad had better have enough thank yous," he said as he eyes did a quick take in of the beautiful woman standing before him and he whistled. They drove silently to Brad's house and she was overwhelmed by the beauty of his mansion when she stepped out. Bradley who had gotten off work early was there to welcome them.

"Hey, I'm Bradley your husband to be and you are Allison I guess," he asked as she bobbed her head in affirmation. He went ahead to let her know her major reason for being there.

"I didn't have the need for a woman in my life few months ago until after my sister's death. Now I brought you here to help me look after Alonzo, her son. I'm sure you are up to the task," he asked and she nodded yet again. "Take very good care of my son, that's one way you can prove that I didn't make the wrong choice. You have to prove your worth." That remark cut through her like a poison laced knife and she turned bitter. She hated being treated that way. Unbeknownst to her, what she had gotten was just the crust of the icing, the cake was yet to be unwrapped.

***

Days later after they were wedded in court as Bradley opted, who literally told her he didn't have money to waste on just a mere help, Allison had already settled in comfortably into her new role as a mother. She was taken by little Alonzo and so her job wasn't so hard as she loved the boy already. She hated it here, she had never felt so lonely in her life. Her husband was hostile and didn't want her butting into his affairs.

"Isn't that what I should be doing as a wife? Trying to help you out with your problems?" She had asked someday after having noticed that he was worried about something.

"That's not what I pay you for lady, it will be really comforting if you stick to your problems." He replied and went back into his room. She had been tempted to call Bonfilio to tell him to pull the plug but something stopped her, the precious little boy resting in his cot before her.

Carter who had noticed how his friend treated her walked into the kitchen while she was preparing dinner for the family and told her that Brad was a nice fellow and could be loving and caring too.

"He has a lot going on at his work place, you have to bear with him," Carter said. Allison knew it wasn't just work. Something was wrong with him as a person and the sooner she found a way out the better.

Allison studied Bradley intently in order to try to understand him. He had a soft spot for Alonzo and his friend Carter. He was actually lovable and looked like the romantic sort if only he could let go and show it. She was gradually falling in love with this stranger that didn't want to have anything to do with her. She was going to get to the bottom of everything. She had to make him fall in love with her somehow, she thought. She went ahead one day to speak with Brad's butler. The old man had been around for quite a while and since they were in good terms, she decided to ask him for advice.

"A nice morning to you Ms. Allison," James replied her greeting. "You look worried, what might the matter be?" He asked.

"I'm worried about me, about Brad. I'm in love with him and it's not helpful that he treats me like some piece of old metal. I figured there's a problem somewhere and since you've been around him for a long while, you could let me know what it is that bugs him so much and why he is the way he is. I see he has a loving heart but barely uses it to love, well except Alonzo and Carter and maybe you. He pushes everyone else away.

"Teach him to open his heart to love. If you really love him, you can find a way around that. You see, Mr. Bradley here doesn't know what it feels like to be loved by any other woman except his late twin sister."

"He was a twin? Oh it must have been painful. Losing your twin? Who could ever recover from that?" She asked as sympathy washed over her.

"What of his mum? She didn't love him?"

"He lost his mum few weeks after she gave birth to them. His old man died later on. So all his life, he's been in charge of things and it has toughened him. He'll get to love, you just have to find the right buttons to press," he finished and left her even more confused than she was earlier.

They've been married for some months now and she barely knew him. She had get to know every detail about this man she wished to have by her side all her life. He was until now a stranger but she hoped to change that story. She started with staying out of his way and just carrying out her duties as Alonzo's mother. She began to throw him nice comments every time he accomplished something. She had Carter to give information of his successes in the factory and she made sure she had his favorite drink out on the table with a note letting him know she was proud of him. She made sure she wasn't around him so much like he requested. He had earlier told her that having her butt into all his affairs was suffocating; he really didn't want to see much of her. But Bradley was beginning to reconsider. *She had only been looking out for you*, Carter's voice reverberated in his mind. Alonzo loved her too at least he could see that from the way he cozied up in her arms every night. He'd rather now sleep with her than in his cot. He was thankful to her for helping him get his freedom to be with friends and still be with Alonzo knowing he was being taken care of enough not to miss out on a mother's love like he did.

Bradley heart constricted with remorse as he stared at the big cake on his table. At first he had walked into a neatly arranged and dust free home which was quiet. He figured they must be asleep and so he just went straight to the room only to find a beautiful cake on his table with his name and Emile's name on it. And a framed childhood picture of he and Emile crested into the cake. He picked up the note with a sentence that thus read, 'she's gone but will forever live in our hearts'

On another note was written 'Happy birthday to this amazing stranger that has taught me what it means to love. I have come to love you Brad and I hope one day, you'll see that I do. I stepped out with Alonzo for a bit, I figured my absence will be one of the best gifts I can give you. I'll have him back for you to celebrate with and Oh Carter will be over later tonight for the party with some friends from work.'

"She's throwing me a party?" He exclaimed with astonishment.

After his sister's death Brad saw no reason to celebrate his birthday especially without Emile. It didn't feel the same anymore but staring at their smiling faces and a picture of Alonzo which was a reminder that not only does Emile live in their hearts, but in that little lovely son of his, the walls of his heart that had been raised to shut Allison out melted and he went to sit at the patio to wait for their return. She was rare and he was lucky to have her. No sane woman would endure the trash he had thrown on her all these while and still stay unless this woman was in love and she was, he was sure of that.

The gate opened and Allison walked in with a sleeping Alonzo. She was surprised to see Bradley charging towards her from the patio. She wondered if she had pressed the wrong button by bringing up Emile's memories on their birthday.

"I'm really sorry Brad. I figured it was one way to help you know she's still with us. I didn't mean to stir up memories you didn't want stirred. I was hurting to see..." She was saying when his lips crashed upon hers. He kissed her with all the passion he could muster. Alonzo stirred in her arms and she pulled away from him.

"I think I'd put him to bed and we can finish what you started," she said with a flirty smile. He followed her in and as soon as he had her to himself ravaged her body with passionate kisses. She let him have her without any reservations. When they were apart and breathing heavily after their first time together, he brought her close to himself. He wanted her always in her arms. He had never had a lady who made him feel secured before now. Ellie had his back but she was the younger of the two and so always needed to be protected. Allison was different. She was caring and a confident woman. He had a lady to show off now at business meetings and at house warming parties. Yet, he had wronged her, he had heaped on her consequences she hadn't merited. Allison wondered what was going on in his head. She had pinched herself until she had nearly drawn blood as she being cuddled by the man that had asked her to stay away from him was too good to be true. He was broken but she promised she wasn't going to fix him. He wasn't some toy or an object that she can pick up and fix whenever it gets broken. She'd rather let him heal and bask in the reflection of her love, that would fix him, she thought.

"I'm sorry Al. Say you've forgiven me please," he pleaded with his eyes.

"I have, even before you asked," she said as she kissed him. She loved this man and she was happy to be his woman.

He wanted a woman who would love him and his son and he just about ordered the perfect woman for the job.

The End...

ONE STARRY NIGHT

LAUREL BIRD

Chapter 1

Carlie watched the front door of her house slam shut. She couldn't help it. She hurried toward it and flung it open again. She saw the male figure walking quickly toward his truck. Carlie grit her teeth and refused to call him back once more.

But try as she might to control her body, she couldn't control the tears that started to stream down her cheeks. He got in his truck, slammed the door shut, and gave her an angry look before starting up his vehicle and squealing away.

"No!" Carlie said. She went in her house and curled up on her couch. This had not been the way it was supposed to go at all. Carlie had been suspected he had been cheating for the last two months, but she had tried to shove her suspicions away. They had been together for two years. She had thought there was no way he would actually cheat on her. She had never thought about cheating on him. Wasn't he just as loyal?

The problem was, what Carlie thought didn't change the facts. Her boyfriend had started yelling at her for snooping on his phone. He hadn't apologized for anything. He said he loved the other girl more anyway. It was just easier to keep Carlie than go through the whole break up. His words echoed through Carlie's head, and the sobs wracked her body again. She felt as if her whole world was falling apart.

"I can't believe this is happening!" Carlie cried in anguish. "I would never do anything like that to him. I thought- I thought he loved me." She shook her head. Her tears would begin to edge away, then a new memory of a comment he had made would flash through her head. "I can't do this," Carlie said pitifully. She wiped her tears away and collapsed on the couch.

Her tired eyes roamed over the living room restlessly. The first thing that caught her eye was a picture of the two of them at their one year anniversary. "No!" Carlie said, grabbed the picture frame and throwing it to the ground. Angry, Carlie threw her heel into it. Then, she turned and walked into the kitchen.

"I don't need him," Carlie said. She thought she had done all her crying when she had first begun suspecting that her boyfriend was cheating, but the sadness still washed over her in waves. "I should get out of here. I need to do something," Carlie said.

She grabbed a canteen and filled it with the hot chocolate she had been making for the two of them. She plopped in a few marshmallows and grabbed a blanket. There was a special spot at the end of the neighborhood. Carlie thought spending some time out under the stars might be good for her soul.

Doubling back into the kitchen, Carlie grabbed her coat from the back hook and put it on. It was promising to be a chilly night, even though it wasn't quite November. Carlie hiked down to the end of the neighborhood. The cold air felt fresh on her face, and she felt determined to enjoy the evening. She was free now. She didn't want to spend the rest of her life with a cheater anyway. It was better that she find out now then later down the line. That would be even more difficult.

Carlie tried to imagine a break up being even more difficult, but she couldn't. Carlie decided to push him out of her mind. She was going to look up at the stars, and. . .

Carlie tried to look up at the stars at that moment, but the street lights were too bright for her to see past them. "I'll see them soon enough," Carlie said to herself.

After about ten more minutes of walking, Carlie reached the end of the neighborhood. The street lights faded behind her as she stepped over the construction tape and climbed a mound to the grassy knoll. She always wanted to come out here and take time to enjoy the beautiful natural surroundings, but in her busy life, she never had time.

Carlie spread her blanket out on the hill and settled onto it, pulling the hot chocolate canteen close to her for warmth. She looked up at the stars and smiled. There were a lot out tonight. Carlie drank a few sips of the hot chocolate but found it was still too hot to drink. She lay down on the blanket and studied the sky. She tried to see if she could find any constellations, but she had never been very good with that sort of thing.

She smiled to herself as her eyes blinked sleepily shut. Suddenly, Carlie was wide awake. She was never sure if she fell asleep or just been drowsy, but she was awake now. Carlie swallowed slowly. What was she doing in the middle of a field? Oh yeah, now she remembered. But, why had she woken up?

Carlie slowly sat up and saw a man standing a few feet away. She opened her mouth and screamed.

Chapter 2

The shadow whipped around to her, and Carlie skittered back a crawl and a tumble. The man's shadow got smaller as he detached himself from another shape that she determined to be a telescope. Carlie studied him as the man came closer.

"Didn't mean to startle you," he said. "But I didn't think I was that ugly."

His attempt at a joke was ignored by Carlie as she sat up and studied him. "What- what are you doing here? Who are you?" When he got closer, Carlie could see that he was quite normal looking. He had glasses and was dressed in long pants and a long collared shirt.

"I'm Matthew," he said, extending his hand. Carlie shook it and invited him to sit on her blanket, never taking her eyes off him.

"Carlie," she said. "I don't you think you live in this neighborhood. I would have met you before, right?"

Matthew shrugged. "I'm from the next neighborhood over. I'm doing some research of the night skies."

Carlie smiled. This guy seemed like the kind of person who would have been called nerd in high school but then grew up to make something of himself. "What are you looking for?"

"Right now, I'm hoping to see Venus and Saturn when they cross orbits."

"Wait, what? Planets cross orbits?" Carlie laughed for the first time since her boyfriend had entered the house that night. "Sorry. I'm not very knowledgeable about that sort of thing. I thought those planets were pretty far apart."

"It's okay," Matthew said. "I'm an astronomer. I want to capture the moment, but I think it might be a few more hours."

"You're going to take a picture?"

"Yes, my telescope can take pictures. This is a fairly common occurrence compared to some others, but I've never been able to see it before. Sometimes, the night is too cloudy or the weather just isn't clear enough for me to catch a glimpse. It looks like tonight will be the night. Sorry," he paused. "I'm just babbling on to you about astronomy, and you're probably bored to death."

"No," Carlie quickly replied. "I don't mind at all. I think it's cool to learn about new things."

"What did you study, if you don't mind my asking, Carlie the mysterious woman who sleeps in the grass?"

Carlie laughed again. "I'm actually an English major."

"Really?" Matthew said. "What do you do?"

"I teach fourth grade. I love kids, so that's my kind of thing," Carlie said. "I thought I might do something a little more aspiring, like be a published author when I got out of school, but that doesn't pay a livable wage."

Matthew leaned back on his elbows. "What would you write about if you could write?"

"Well," Carlie paused. "I do write, actually. I just don't. . .publish it."

"Why not?" Matthew asked. Carlie felt odd that this stranger was so interested in her life, but he seemed nice enough. He wasn't trying to harass her; he was just trying to pass the hours until his special moment came.

Carlie shrugged, taking the time to evaluate why she wasn't pursuing what she loved. "It's a hard world to publish in. I'd have to pay an agent, and then companies could still reject my manuscripts. Besides, I don't know if they're really anything someone would want to read. They're more like things I write to help me process what's going on in my life."

"Like a journal," Matthew added.

"Sure, like a journal, except," Carlie's voice caught, and she muffled the sound with a sip from her hot chocolate. "Things always end happily."

Matthew looked at her. "Wouldn't that be great if life could always end just like we wanted it to?"

Carlie nodded. "In a book, no matter what hard times characters go through, they are still happy in the end."

"You know what's terrible," Matthew said, making Carlie look at him sharply. Matthew was the kind of guy who made you want to listen to what he was going to say. "In books, the story always ends just as characters are getting to that happy place in their lives. You see that as a good thing. I don't. I think it's better if they get to live out a bit of that happiness and not just have it in the end. It's like the eating the worst food you have ever eaten to be rewarded with a big chocolate cake in the end. But you only get to have half a bite."

Carlie laughed and lay back on the blanket. "Wow, you're going to make me think you're crazy. I never looked at it that way before."

"We're always in search of a happy ending, so busy looking for that happy ending, that we don't take the time right now to enjoy the happiness we already have."

"Where do all of these brilliant ideas come from?" Carlie asked.

Matthew laughed, and Carlie liked the sound of his laughter. It was deep and genuine. "My many, many years of experience."

Carlie looked around at him. "Oh, you're not so old. How old are you?"

"Twenty-nine," Matthew said. Carlie nodded. He was three years older than she was. Matthew pressed his watch, and it lit up. "I think it should happen in another hour."

Carlie smiled, but a little bit of her didn't want to end their conversation. She was having such a great time trading ideas with him.

"What brought you out here tonight?" Matthew asked. "You know what I'm doing, but I don't know what you're doing."

Carlie shrugged. "Sometimes, I just want to be close to nature and enjoy its beauty."

Matthew raised his eyebrows. "Alright. I'll assume you know how to do that while sleeping, then."

Carlie laughed and pushed his shoulder with her own. "Stop it! I didn't mean to sleep. That just happened. Besides, I had plenty of time to enjoy nature's beauty before I fell asleep."

Matthew smiled. "I'll be right back." He went over to his telescope and adjusted a few things, then he grabbed his bag and brought it over to the edge of the blanket. "Are you hungry?"

"That depends on what you have," Carlie said. "If it's something delicious, then I'm always ready for some of that."

Matthew smiled and took out a bag of chips and a container of fruit salad. "I don't know if this is what you would consider delicious, but it's junky and healthy at the same time, so that's what I chose to bring."

"Thanks," Carolyn said, taking the container's lid that Matthew had liberally sprinkled with fruit. "Here, I have hot chocolate if you want some."

They sat on the blanket sharing the food and hot chocolate, silent under the stars. Carlie glanced over at Matthew. The only light came from the stars, so she couldn't see him very well. What she did know was that no matter what he looked like, he was the kind of person that made you want to be around him.

"Oh!" Matthew jumped up after looking at his watch. "I need to go monitor my telescope!"

Chapter 3

Carlie watched as Matthew hurried away. He had a notebook, and he was furiously taking notes, though how he could see them was a mystery to Carlie. She watched him work and wondered what it would be like to know everything about the stars and to understand how the planets revolved.

"Carlie!" Matthew called, his voice seeming crude in the calm air. "Don't you want to come see?"

Of course, she did! Carlie jumped up, throwing a few pieces of fruit to the ground accidentally, and rushed over to Matthew's side.

"Okay, they're going to cross in about five minutes, so I'll need to be looking through at that point to take the pics. But I thought you might want to see them."

"Which planets? And what do they look like?"

"Saturn and Venus."

"They cross paths?" Carlie asked again, puzzled.

"Quick," Matthew said. He placed his hand on her arm and pulled her toward the telescope. "I'll explain to you afterward."

Carlie laughed and looked through the telescope, searching for something that she would call a planet.

"They're going to look like large stars, nothing more," Matthew instructed. "They should be centered in the telescope."

Carlie jumped back as though the telescope had stung her. "Hey! I saw them, but they're super close. You better get in there or you're going to miss them."

Matthew pressed his eye against the glass and began changing the telescope. Carlie heard a clicking noise, and she assumed he was taking pictures of the planets. She waited patiently until the deed was done. Matthew turned away from the telescope with a huge smile on his face.

"I got it," he said. "Did you see that?"

Carlie nodded, even though she had not understood exactly what she had seen. "That's awesome! I'm glad," Carlie said, nodding enthusiastically.

Matthew sighed then looked at Carlie. He seemed to realize that his goal was completed. Carlie wondered if he was going to pack up and leave. He had no other reason to stay.

"We should probably eat up that fruit," Matthew said. "It'll just go bad anyway if I take it home."

Carlie went back to the blanket and gathered the fruit that had fallen on the blanket. It was still good. She slowly forked each piece of fruit into her mouth. She wanted to ask Matthew more about his job, what he did, and his life, but the conversation felt awkward now.

"I guess you've got school tomorrow," Matthew finally said, as Carlie was finishing up her fruit.

"No," Carlie said. "It's Labor Day. That means vacation. You're not working tomorrow, or are you?"

Matthew gave her a startled look. "Well, science doesn't exactly work on the same schedule. I'll probably go into the office even though it's Labor Day. I might as well get some work done."

Carlie nodded. "So you're a workaholic then?"

Matthew grinned at her. "You write when you get home from school. Does that make you a workaholic?"

Carlie laughed. "Okay, you got me. We'll just settle it that we are both NOT workaholics. Deal?" She offered her hand to Matthew who took it, but he didn't shake it. Instead, he pulled her to her feet.

"Ready to go home?" he asked.

Carlie sighed and glanced down at the blanket that had offered her comfort for the last few hours. She decided that once Matthew had packed up, she would stay for a time more. Maybe she would sleep outside for the night. Carly smiled. "I think I'm going to stay a little longer."

"I was just thinking the same thing," Matthew said. "I'm not quite ready to go yet."

Carlie looked over at Matthew and made eye contact. His two pools of eyes, too dark to really make out were looking right back at her. Carlie's stomach rolled over.

"Do you want to explore?" Carlie asked. "I used to know these woods when I was a little girl. I can show you some pretty cool things."

"You lived here when you were a kid?" Matthew asked her.

Carlie shook her head. "Ironically, my best friend grew up in a house on this street. I came over here all the time. When I moved in here, it felt like I was moving into a familiar glove, not a new one that's all difficult to break in. Come on."

"I have a penlight if it'll help," Matthew said, leaving a cover on his telescope so that it would be protected from any possible rain. "I think we should be safe. The skies are clear."

Carlie smiled at him and pulled him away from the open meadow and into the trees. She released his hand once they were under the trees. The darkness had engulfed them.

"I assume you know where we're going, right?" Matthew said, teasing Carlie.

"No," she said. "Let's get lost." She grabbed his hand again, a total sense of abandon coming over her. She felt like a child again, throwing all of her worries to the wind as she picked her way along the barely visible path. "I don't think as many kids have been playing here now," Carlie said. "This path used to be wider and clearer."

"Probably has to do with the 'No Trespassing' sign in the front of this area."

Carlie shrugged. "Yeah, you're probably right. Good thing you and I are both daredevils." Carlie glanced down at their clasped hands, and a sick feeling cut through her. What was she trying to prove? She was flirting with a man she had just met, and. . .

Carlie looked up into Matthew's eyes again. She could see his white smile clearly shining in the dark. "You seem a little lost to me," Matthew said.

Carlie turned away from him, dropping his hand again. "No, I know exactly where I'm going, but I think you have a problem trusting me to guide you."

Matthew laughed. "Sure, think I'm strange because I have trouble trusting a woman I just met on a dark night."

Carlie joined his laughter. "You make me sound like a strange witch that appeared out of nowhere. Did you see me when you were setting up?"

"Well, even if I had been blind, I would have heard your snoring," Matthew said.

Carlie gave him a horrified look. "No! I wasn't snoring. Please tell me you are making that up." Matthew gave an impish shrug, and Carlie pushed his chest. "You big tease. I knew I didn't snore."

"I never said I was making it up," Matthew said. "Anyway, I wasn't going to wake you up, and there is no other place as good as that one for watching the planets."

Carlie nodded and led him forward. "Why don't you go first?" she suggested. "You have the light."

"Where is it that we're going?" Matthew asked.

Carlie smiled. That was her secret. He would find out soon enough.

"Be patient. Wait, and you will see."

"Alright," Matthew said, "But if I lead us the wrong way, it's not my fault."

Carlie stood aside and let him pass her on the small path. She got behind him and started following his tall figure as they worked their way over the childhood path.

"Looks like we've come to a fork," Matthew said. "Which way?"

"Right," Carlie said. They were almost there.

"Did you and your friend make this path?" Matthew asked.

Carlie nodded. "Yeah, we spent multiple days using a broom and picking out rocks, etc. Then, we walked on it so much, that it kind of became part of the forest."

"Sounds like a fun childhood," Matthew said. "I always wanted to be that sort of kid, but I was always the kid who stayed inside and played with Legos. Now, I stay inside all day and play with telescopes and star charts."

"Have you come to your happy ending?" Carlie asked, remembering their conversation from earlier.

Matthew raised his eyebrows. "I hope I haven't come to an ending, happy or not. I'm not ready for my life to be over yet."

"Guess you shouldn't have come into the woods with a strange woman then," Carlie said, laughing maniacally. Matthew turned to her and shone the light on his face to show his horror stricken expression.

"Hey, I have the light," he said. "I can leave you behind in the darkness to consider your evil behavior."

Carlie laughed again. "Oh, Matthew, you wouldn't dare. I can already tell you're too much of a gentleman."

Matthew turned and looked at her for a moment before he continued walking.

"There it is," Carlie said, pointing into the trees ahead. The ropes were a little older than she had remembered them. Even though she had moved into the neighborhood, she hadn't brought herself to visit their homemade ropes course and fort since she was fifteen or sixteen.

"Whoa!" Matthew said. "You made this?"

Carlie nodded. "My friend and her dad helped. I promise you; it's safe. At least, it was safe ten years ago."

Matthew went over and tugged on one of the ropes. It seemed to be holding on strong. "I know you say it's safe, and it feels nice and strong. But," Matthew shook his head. "I don't know I would risk my life on a dark night trying it out."

A little part of Carlie felt disappointed. She had wanted to return to her childhood. She had wanted to feel that free of worry again. But, she found that even without mounting the course, she still felt happier than she had in a long time.

"Paula and I used to do it all the time. We would time each other and see who was the fastest."

Matthew was examining the course piece by piece. "I think I missed out on this piece of my childhood," he said, smiling back at her. Carlie loved the way his teeth lit up in the dark.

"Look," Carlie said. "You can at least trust the swing, right?"

Matthew went over to the swing and pushed on it. It seemed trustworthy. "Let's sit," Matthew said, gesturing toward the bench.

Chapter 4

Carlie sat down on the bench next to Matthew and found herself automatically snuggling up to him, not that she usually snuggled up to strangers. It was just that he felt so comfortable, and familiar in an odd sort of way. Matthew put his arm around her, and Carlie smiled.

"I heard a quote, and I was just thinking about it," Carlie said, meditating deep things as Matthew clicked off the penlight and the sound of crickets began to fill the air. "It said, 'Was it really a bad day or was it just a bad five minutes that you milked all day?' Sometimes, I let bad things take over my life. It's hard not to blow them out of proportion."

Matthew's hand was slowly stroking Carlie's hair. It didn't feel strange at all. She felt as if she had known him for years. "I suffer the same. I think it's normal. You have to decide to be happy."

Carlie smiled and turned toward Matthew. "And right now, that decision isn't so hard. I'm deciding to be happy." She smiled at Matthew, and she could see him smiling back at her. "I guess I realized I don't need much to be happy."

"What do you need to be happy?" Matthew asked.

"Right now? All it took was a beautiful night, a blanket, and a strange man looking at the stars."

Matthew laughed. Carlie looked at him and felt an urge to kiss him. She wondered what his lips tasted like. Not hesitating at all, Carlie leaned forward, her eyes fluttering closed. She gently pressed her lips against his, and he leaned into her. Carlie felt the sparks fly as they kissed. She suddenly pulled back, her heart racing. Her breath was coming quickly as she looked at Matthew in a new light.

Carlie swallowed carefully and lay her head back on Matthew's chest, turning her mind back to the stars and the planets and other things.

"You're certainly not what I was expecting when I planned to go out stargazing tonight," Matthew said. Carlie's smile was sweet.

"You weren't what I was expecting either," Carlie replied. Carlie squinted as Matthew suddenly pulled out his phone and the bright light flared up. Matthew pressed a few buttons on his phone, and soft music began to play. It wasn't the sort of music Carlie had ever kept on her phone. It was the type of music that had lyrics that made you think, not lyrics that made you want to start dancing like crazy.

"You're a very deep man," Carlie said as she evaluated his music choice.

"Does that mean I'm hard to figure out?" Matthew asked.

Carlie shrugged. "I don't really know what to make of you. You're. . .I don't know. I feel like I could tell you anything."

"Tell me anything then," Matthew said. "I'm ready to listen."

Carlie sighed. "The truth is that I don't want reality to hit me."

"Are you running from something?"

"Pain, a lot of pain. I came out here to try to escape, even if I wasn't thinking that when I came. I didn't think I'd find someone to escape with."

"Where are we going?" Matthew asked. "If we're escaping, we should go somewhere good, where we wouldn't mind hiding for a while."

"Hawaii," Carlie said, the first tropical place that popped into her mind.

"Hawaii it is then," Matthew said, his hand resting across her shoulders and on her upper arm. "I love the beaches and the sound of the waves."

Carlie closed her eyes and imagined they were sitting on the edge of the beach, her toes ready to dig into the sand. "It would be warmer," she said. "We would dive into the cold water and feel refreshed."

"There would be seashells on the beach. I have a huge collection of shells. I still need a perfect conch, though."

"There's going to be the perfect conch shell there," Carlie said. "Warm sand, and cold water. A beautiful sunset with an array of colors. Oh, I wish I could be there right now." Carlie opened her eyes to the chilly weather and the dark night and felt disappointed. She felt as though her night had been a little spoiled.

"Come on," Matthew said, standing and fully bringing Carlie out of her imagination. "Let's go."

"Where to?" Carlie crinkled her nose.

"I too may have my share of secrets," Matthew announced.

Carlie laughed. "What do you know about these woods?"

"I didn't say it had to do with these woods," Matthew said, taking Carlie's hand. He led her through the dark, following the path. Carlie held his hand tightly. She told herself it was for warmth, but in reality, Matthew was tugging at more than just her hand. He had a grip on her attention, and Carlie didn't seem able to pull it away.

Out under the stars once again, Matthew turned to Carlie and took both of her hands. Carlie laughed aloud. She hadn't felt this happy and free since she was a child. Carlie broke away from one of Matthew's hands and pulled him up the hill at a running pace. Closing her eyes,

Carlie pulled Matthew close and began swaying to the music he still had playing softly from his pocket.

Matthew laughed his low laugh and squeezed her tightly. They swayed back and forth to the music, then Matthew tried to spin Carlie away from him. It didn't work as well as he had been planning it, and Carlie tumbled to the ground. She laughed as she looked up at Matthew who was looking quite embarrassed.

"I guess you can tell I haven't had much practice dancing. Brooms turn a lot easier you know."

Carlie laughed and reached up for the hand Matthew was offering her. "I guess I'll have to help you get some practice in," Carlie said.

Matthew held her close. "I'd like that," he whispered. Carlie cuddled up to him as they danced, slowly moving back and forth. The music and the swaying movement made Carlie realize how tired she was. She didn't want the night to end, though, and she forced herself to stay awake.

"Are you ready to practice that spin again?" Matthew asked.

Carlie nodded and followed Matthew's lead. He dipped her, and Carlie saw the world upside down for a few moments before he brought her back up. She smiled at him. "You're a good dancer," she said, just as the song ended.

"That is definitely a first," Matthew said. "I've never heard those words before, at least not directed at me."

"They should have been," Carlie said.

Matthew raised his eyebrows. "Because I'm excellent at throwing girls on the floor?"

His question hung in the air, and they both started laughing.

"Well," Carlie said. "You've already brushed up on that skill, and your others are all excellent."

Matthew hugged Carlie tightly. "Thanks. That's really sweet of you."

"I think my legs are getting tired," Carlie said. "Do you need to go back?" What she really wanted to do was plead him to stay with her just a little longer. She wasn't ready for their night to end. She wanted to spend just a little more time with this man who had challenged her generic perspective on life.

Chapter 5

"I can stay a little bit longer, but then I should really get to sleep. You too," Matthew said as they walked over to the blanket. Carlie collapsed onto it. It didn't feel nearly as warm as she had remembered it. She knew their time was ticking away, and she wanted to just stop the clock. She didn't know what time it was, and she didn't want to know either. She avoided looking at Matthew's watch when he lit it up. "It's-"

"Stop! I don't want to know," Carlie said as Matthew sat then lay next to her. "I don't want to crash into reality yet. I just want to remain in our little paradise a little longer."

Matthew put his arm around her and pulled her close. Carlie curled her legs up and leaned against him. "Why are you so scared of going back into reality?"

Matthew's words were searching for truth, and Carlie was too scared to give it to him. "I- I have a lot going on right now. I don't want to enter reality and feel the same emotions I was feeling earlier. It's better here." Carlie had split the two in her mind, and she didn't want the magical night to end.

Matthew kissed Carlie's hair gently, and it made her smile up at the stars.

"I'm sorry," he said.

Carlie closed her eyes. "it's not your fault. Life is like that, huh? It throws you curveballs just to make sure you still know how to jump."

"Good thing you can still jump," Matthew said, kissing her hair again.

"I think I'm crippled," Carlie said, the tears coming to her eyes as the pain of the encounter, which now seemed days ago, hit her again.

Matthew saw up and looked at her. He saw the tears and gently wiped the away.

"Nothing can cripple you forever unless you let it. Do you understand? You are in charge of your life."

Carlie knew his words were meant to be encouraging, but she just felt too sad to be encouraged back to a smile. She sat up and folded herself into Matthew's arms. Her tears came. They weren't ugly sobs that racked her whole body but silent streams that blinded her. When she seemed to have nothing left, she sat back. "You're a brave one," she said to Matthew. "You're not scared off by anything."

"I generally like to think I'm not a scaredy-cat."

Carlie burst into a smile that caused a snot bubble to blow out of her nose. Carlie was embarrassed as she wiped it away. She turned her face away, but Matthew was smiling down on her, not the kind of mean smile but a gentle, teasing smile.

"I'm still not scared," Matthew said.

"You should probably take the warnings and run far away," Carlie warned. But even she did not take her own advice. She leaned against Matthew again. The stars seemed different. Did they change during the night? She started to ask Matthew, but she knew he might go down a long astronomical explanation that would confuse more than help her. She just sat, letting her thoughts wash over her.

Her eyes started closing, and she felt as though she could go to sleep right there. Matthew suddenly moved, causing her to startle and sit up. "I have one thing I want to show you," Matthew said. He pulled his bag a few inches closer and rustled around. Carlie sat up and tried to orient herself.

Matthew pulled out a stone from his bag. He admired the stone for a minute then passed it on to Carlie. Carlie looked at it. "What is it?" she asked. That answer was obvious. Her real question was why was he showing her this thing.

"It's a stone from a meteorite," Matthew said.

Carlie's eyebrows rose. "A real meteorite?"

"No," Matthew said. "The fake one that landed a few towns over and made a massive hole."

"When did that happen?" Carlie handled the stone, fingering its curves and edges.

"It was before we were both born, but it's still there off the edge of town."

"I don't know how I never heard of that," Carlie said.

"This stone reminds me that we're so small. The world, the planets, the solar systems, are enormous. Our little lives are nothing in comparison. It helps remind me that my problems will pass. Why don't you keep it?"

Carlie nodded. "Thank you." She pocketed the stone. It felt warm in her pocket.

"We should probably go," Matthew said, standing and pulling her to her feet.

Carlie rubbed her eyes and stood stupidly for a few minutes as she tried to wake up. When she was able to function, she gathered her blanket and handed Matthew his things to put in his bag. Once she had her canteen, Carlie was ready to go. She watched Matthew pack up his telescope and stow it carefully in the back of his car. Finally, Matthew shut the door, and Carlie knew what came now.

"I can drive you to your house," Matthew said. "Where do you live?"

Carlie smiled, but she shook her head. "Thanks, but I'd like to walk. It's not far. I live just up this street."

Matthew nodded. He took a step forward then paused. "Maybe, I don't know. I'd. . .like your number. Can I?" Carlie slowly nodded. He pulled out his phone and typed the number in. He tucked his phone away, and they both looked at each other awkwardly.

Finally, Matthew took a step forward, and Carlie turned her lips up toward him. He kissed her gently, just as softly as a whisper of wind.

As he stepped back, Carlie wanted to pull him toward her again, but she didn't. She watched him get in his car and start it up. The two red taillights faded into the distance, and Carlie was alone again.

She began the walk back to her house, back to reality, the warmth of Matthew's hand and kiss still lingering on her. Carlie wondered if in the morning light, her magical night would have disappeared. Would Matthew be the same person she had met on the grassy knoll? Was she even the same person she had been tonight?

Carlie hadn't felt the need to hide herself from Matthew. He was completely real. Carlie climbed into her bed, spreading the blanket from the meadow on her, not caring about the bits of grass. Sometimes, fantasy is better than reality.

The scent of Matthew's cologne lingered on the blanket, and as Carlie fell into her dreams, she knew that Mathew was the kind of man worth being real for.

IMPERFECT

Amy's favorite thing about her job at the travel agency was her headset. It was outdated, and half the time she couldn't hear anything but static coming from the other end, but it was *big* and that was enough. The silver earpiece jutted out to cover half of her cheek, and the adjustable mike was enough to distract from the rest. She kept it on even when she wasn't making calls to airlines or bus stations; in the past few months, the awkward metal piece had become more and more of a security blanket to her while she worked. With it on, she didn't have to worry about the stares, or the questions, or the laughter that always seemed to be directed at her.

Today, she was especially grateful for the distraction. She had overslept, and hadn't had time to apply the thick foundation that she used to obscure the dark purple stains of her birthmark that covered most of the lower left half of her face. For the first five hours of her shift, she hunched behind the tall desk in the front office of the Del Casa Travel Agency, taking phone calls and hoping—*praying*—that they wouldn't have any walk-ins before her lunch break.

She was lucky—mid-winter wasn't exactly the busiest time of year. The only visitor—and not even a *real* visitor—was her roommate, Lena, who came by to bring Amy her much-needed morning coffee, and to make sure that their plans were still in place for that night.

"I promise, you'll love it," Lena said as she handed Amy her steaming mug. Amy sniffed it gingerly and took a precautionary sip as she raised an eyebrow. Lena shrugged her pretty shoulders and tossed her snow-damp mane of golden hair over her shoulder. She was the exact opposite of her friend and housemate—where Lena was tan, Amy was pale; where Lena was bright and wild, Amy was...not. By all accounts—friends and family alike—they should not have gotten along with each other. But, as Amy had read in a book once, if the sun and moon could share the sky, she and Lena could be friends. Even if they didn't necessarily agree on the same things.

"No offense meant to you," Amy said gently, "but God and I aren't exactly simpatico at the moment." In fact, she couldn't remember a time when they really had been. She could remember going to church a few times when she was a child, but the barrage of elderly women patting her cheek and calling her "poor, sweet girl," and asking quietly if she wanted them to pray for her, had quickly doused any spark of enthusiasm that she had possessed for the local diocese. Until she'd met Lena—devout Catholic wondergirl—she hadn't even really considered religion on a regular basis. To Amy, worship was something that other people did. People that were...not like her.

"You'll at least like the building," Lena pleaded. After months of wheedling, she had finally worn Amy down into agreeing to go on a night visit to a church with her. "It's old—with the stained class and the vaulted ceilings, just like those ones in Italy that you're always looking at."

Amy sipped at her coffee and shrugged.

"It's not mass, so we'll probably be the only people there. Come on, you promised."

"You know how I do in public places," Amy said. "I just...I don't think I'd be very comfortable, and it's been a rough week as it is..."

"That's why you *should* come, though," Lena said, leaning back on the rickety old desktop of the Del Casa foyer. "This one church is the most peaceful, accepting place that I've ever set foot in. Nobody'll even look at you twice. And if they do—" she leaned forward, her eyes narrowing. "—they'll have me to deal with. You won't be alone this time."

'This time' referred back to the weekend walk that Amy had taken the weekend before, in an attempt to get *some* semblance of exercise, only to be verbally assaulted by a crowd of teenage boys smoking on the street corner. She hadn't cried about it when she'd returned home, but Lena—sensitive friend that she was—had known something had happened and tugged the story out of Amy as soon as she'd been calm enough to speak.

It was Lena's loyalty that won Amy over in the end—she'd done so much for her friend, and never let her down. It really was the least Amy could do, to give in to this one small, well-meaning demand.

X

Amy didn't dress up. She'd always been more of a jeans-and-t-shirt kind of girl, anyway, and the idea of wearing a dress and having to do something more with her hair—something that would, very possibly, reveal more of the purple birthmark as it spread down her cheek and curled around her neck—did nothing but cause her chest to tighten. The church was just as magnificent as Lena had promised—it had been built like one of those big medieval cathedrals, complete with stone spires and sparkling glass windows.

She followed her roommate inside, but took care to keep her eyes down as they passed a priest, and then a man who looked like a gardener. So much for an empty chapel.

"If you want," Lena whispered as they filed down an aisle between the uncomfortable-looking wooden pews, "You can take a seat. I'm going to light a candle for Grandma and pray for a while before I go to confessional."

Amy glanced around the spacious room. The few people that were there with them were either kneeling before the rack of glowing candles that burned beneath the feet of a smiling statue of a woman, or sitting in the pews near the back.

"I'll be sitting over here," she said, pointing to an empty pew away from any strange eyes. "Let me know when you're finished."

"Thanks, Amy." Lena grinned and patted her friend's shoulder before trotting back down the aisle towards the flickering lights.

Amy settled—as much as she could—into the cold wooden seat, and shoved her chilly hands into the deep pockets of her jacket. She craned her neck to watch Lena light a match and bow over a mostly unlit section of the candle board. The priest that they had passed outside appeared at her roommate's elbow and placed a hand on Lena's shoulder. They exchanged greetings.

Somehow, Amy had the feeling that agreeing to attend an actual mass might have been a better idea. At least then, she wouldn't be stuck sitting for another hour and a half.

She was twisting in her seat, trying to count the number of biblical references apparent in the stained glass windows, when she heard the heavy wooden doors of the chapel swing open, and the metallic clacking of *something* against the floor. She stopped twisting and settled back in her seat, focusing her eyes firmly on the next pew ahead, determined not to attract any attention. That was one skill that she'd perfected—the art of controlled invisibility.

"Excuse me," someone said. It was a nice voice, Amy thought. Deep and calm, but friendly. "Excuse me, miss?"

"Oh," Amy gasped, and sat up. "You're talking to me."

"Yes," the man said. He was tall and muscular, with a sharp jaw and cheekbones that were just visible beneath the solid black sunglasses that he wore. He had on a fitted gray suit, and sported a five-o'clock shadow. In his hands he held a long aluminum cane.

"Oh," Amy blurted. "You're—"

"Devastatingly handsome?" The blind man grinned, revealing two rows of white teeth, and Amy's breath caught in her throat because...well, because he was. Devastatingly handsome, that is. "I was just wondering if I could sit here."

"O-of...I mean, of course." Amy said, and slid down a few inches to give him room.

He sat, and crossed his legs as he collapsed the cane in his hands and tucked it into a pocket on the inside of his coat. The glasses came off too, and Amy—who, she wasn't even really ashamed to admit, was openly staring—revealed a pair of unfocused but brilliantly blue eyes.

"I've never met you before," the man said after a moment of silence. He shifted his body towards Amy. "Are you new to the faith?"

"Uh," Amy cleared her throat again. "Not really. My friend...she's really into this place, and she's been wanting to bring me since I'm not exactly faithful...and I finally had a free night to come along."

"Exciting," the man said, and Amy laughed out loud at the sarcasm that dripped from that one word alone.

"Tell me about it," she said. "What about you?"

"I've got a brother in the choir," he said, and uncrossed his very long legs. "I come here sometimes to listen to them practice."

"Oh," Amy said. "That's nice."

"It is," he said. "What's your name?"

She told him.

"Amy," he said slowly, rolling the name around on his tongue. "I like that."

"S-so do I," she stuttered. "I mean, it belongs to me, and..."

He laughed. "Then it means even more that you like it. I hate my name, and I'm stuck with it."

"Oh? What's your name?"

"You'll laugh."

"It can't be that bad."

"You'd be surprised."

Amy turned to face the stranger. "Try me."

He smiled again, and Amy bit back a groan. *That's a smile,* she thought, *That's a smile that will get me into a lot of trouble if I let it.*

But then, just as his mouth opened, and he began to breathe out the first syllable of his name, the spell was broken.

"Ames," Lena called from the other end of the pew. "Ready to go?"

"I'll see you later," the stranger said as she stood and buttoned her coat again.

"Yeah," She said. "Nice talking to you."

The walk home was less then exciting. Lena had gone from respectful worshipper to curious friend the moment they exited the building.

"He was *hot*," were the first words out of his mouth. "I can't believe you were talking to him."

"Thanks." Amy rolled her eyes, but stifled a smile.

"Well, you know what I mean. You're not exactly a social butterfly, babe."

"He started it."

"Ah." Lena galloped a few steps ahead. "The truth comes out."

"I don't know, I just...felt rude not saying anything back."

"And he didn't say anything about your face?"

That made Amy wince. Lena was a fantastic roommate, but she was anything but blunt.

"Well," she said slowly, "considering the fact that he's blind, I don't think that was a huge factor."

Lena paused for a moment before falling back into step beside her roommate. "A blind guy. A hot blind guy."

"Lena..."

"It just keeps getting better. Plus, I heard you laugh all the way in the confessional booth thing. Whatever they call it."

"Do you know when the boy's choir practices?"

"Yeah. Tuesdays and Thursdays, seven to nine. Why?"

"His brother's in it. That's why he comes....or, came, tonight. To listen."

"I think I can fit some mild sin into my week so we can swing by for confessional again. If that's what you're hinting at."

"It might be."

"Aw!" Lena turned in a circle. "Look at my baby Ames. Growing up, getting ready to leave the nest and finally talk to strangers..."

"You know, that's something most pseudo-moms would discourage."

"I'm very open minded. Now, tell me everything he said. Word for word."

The rest of the week passed slowly. Amy's work at the travel agency had slowed so much that she began devoting a good portion of time to cleaning and organizing her workspace, and shooting up a rare prayer or two that business would pick up soon so she wouldn't get the sack. All the while—through tedious holiday calls to distant relatives and trudging journeys to the subway—the memory of the blind man's smile lingered in the back of her mind. When Tuesday rolled around again, she found herself straightening her hair (for once) and brushing her teeth more attentively than usual. Just in case.

Lena skipped happily next to her on the way to church, and talked about her day to distract Amy from the nerve-wracking possibility of interacting with the stranger again.

"So I told the manager, "I hope you don't kiss your mom with that mouth," and he started laughing so hard that I just left, Amy, I just left," Lena pushed open the church door. "...and you're not listening to me."

"Ha ha."

"Well, I thought it was funny." Lena shrugged. "Hey, you want me to light a candle for your love life?"

"Is that a thing?" Amy asked. "Because if that's a thing that you can do, I will take full advantage of it."

"I can always ask." Lena winked. "We're a little early. Sure you don't want to pray with me?"

"Not my thing, remember?"

"It's people like you that made Jesus cry."

"Wow, Len."

"See, that? That's something I'm gonna have to confess. See what you do to me?"

"I'm such a bad influence." Amy stopped halfway down the aisle. "This is my spot."

"Someone's been overthinking."

"I don't get to flirt often."

"All right," Lena grinned. "Give him hell."

"Just try not to get struck by lightning while I'm working my magic."

Lena walked away shaking her head and laughing to herself. Amy settled back in the pew to wait.

It actually wasn't a bad church, she decided as she propped one arm up against the wooden back rest. The windows were pretty, and the haze of candle smoke passing through fluorescent light almost looked romantic. She almost didn't take notice of the telltale metallic clacking of the aluminum cane.

"Do my senses deceive me, or has the mysterious Amy returned?"

She smiled as he took his seat. "You sense correctly, oh wise and powerful one."

"Well, I don't know so much about wise, but I'm definitely okay with being called powerful," he said. "Got a nice ring to it."

"It'll work for now," Amy said. "At least, until you decide to tell me your name."

"Oh," he pulled off his glasses. "Right."

"I can think of a billion really bad names, and there's next to no chance that you'll have any of them."

"What's at the top of the list?"

"A classic." Amy scooted a little closer along the pew. "Rumplestiltskin."

A bark of real laughter escaped his lips and echoed off of the stone columns that supported the arching ceiling.

"Okay," he admitted. "That was good."

"Will you tell me now?"

He thought about that for a minute. "I will...in exchange for something."

"I'm not going to sell you my firstborn, if that's what you're talking about."

"No," he held up his hands in front of him. "Nothing like that. I'll tell you my name...if you promise to tell me what you look like."

"Oh."

"Oh?"

"I mean..." Amy cleared her throat. "I mean, I'm not that good at describing things, it probably won't be that interesting..." Her hand flew up to rest against the skin of her neck; skin that she knew was dark and blotchy and *ugly*.

"Humor me," he said, and leaned forward. "You smell like new rain and paper and ink. Your voice could belong to a professional rhetorician; it's so well put together. And I'm curious."

"I," Amy stammered, "I don't...okay."

"Good," he said seriously, and extended a hand to her. "Albion Dominic Borzoni, at your service."

Amy took his hand. "It's not that bad."

"I can hear you laughing."

"*Albion*." Amy giggled. "It sounds like something out of a fantasy novel."

"Romance, actually. My mother is a fan." He shrugged. "Now...describe for me."

"What do you want to know?"

"What you want to tell me," he said. "And...you can just call me Al."

"Okay." Amy frowned. "Well, I've got...brown hair. Curly. It almost reaches my shoulders now, but when I straighten it, it's longer. I've got hazel eyes and a pointy chin, and I'm a little overweight if I'm being honest..."

"Good," he said, tilting his handsome head upward. "I can picture it."

"I have all my teeth..."

"Sounds like something that a girl without all her teeth would say...but go on."

"I'm about five and a half feet tall, so a lot shorter than you…I think. And I have a wide mouth. A tiny little nose. Big eyes. Like a mouse."

"A very sweet mouse."

"A-and I have two piercings on each ear. I'm wearing a gold stud and a silver hoop on each. I have…long fingers. No rings. I used to play the piano and I hated the way they clacked against the keys whenever I wore them." Amy glanced upward, and felt her cheeks heat up. Al was facing towards her, eyes cast downward, but he sat completely still, at attention. She knew that she was being listened to.

"I have…smooth skin, I think. Except for a few acne scars on my face, and…and…" her hand went again to her throat. "And that's it. I think."

"What a beautiful image," Al said after a moment of absorbing silence. "You do that very well."

"Thank you."

"Would it be rude of me to ask if I could touch you?"

"E-excuse—"

"Just your face. To get a clearer image of you."

"Oh." Amy relaxed. "Yeah. I guess."

"Fantastic." Al held out his hands in front of him. "If you could…"

"Absolutely." Amy grasped his wrists in her hands and guided his fingers to her forehead. They brushed her skin gently, smoothly, as they worked their way from her hairline to the smallest crevice in her chin. She hoped that he couldn't feel her heart racing in her chest.

"It's just the way you described it," he said when he had finished. "Beautiful. Amazing."

It was the former word that stuck in Amy's mind as she walked home that night with Lena.

"He felt your face," her roommate said. "He felt your *face* and all you can worry about is that you forgot to tell him about your birthmark."

"I didn't forget," she hissed. "Lena, I didn't forget. I...I cut it out. I didn't want him to see it as part of me, so I...lied."

"Honey..."

"He called me beautiful, and I lied to him."

"It's not a big deal. The next time you see him, you can just say 'hey, hot blind guy, I forgot to tell you that I have this really cool birthmark that covers half of my face.'" Lena shrugged. "Problem solved. Did you at least get his number?"

"I was too worried to ask."

"Girl, I swear..."

"Can you swear after I've gone to bed, Len? I'm exhausted."

"You know, one day we are going to have a good girl chat. About feelings. It's going to happen, and you're going to love it."

"I know I will, but I'm so tired and pissed off right now..."

"No worries, hon," Lena said gently. "We'll figure something out."

The best solution, Amy decided, would be to never see Al again. It wouldn't be that hard—they'd only ever met at the church, he didn't know her full name, they'd never talked about anything incredibly personal...It was a foolproof plan.

"I don't like it," was all Lena said in response to her roommate's decision. "Avoiding him won't make the problem go away. I see why you're doing it and I'm not going to pressure you at all. But I don't like it."

And she didn't.

Another week passed, and Amy worked—hard. She scrubbed the office down, did the apartment dishes, organized her closet by color. But that didn't keep her from waiting in the front room for Lena to return from her confessional that Tuesday.

"He was there," Lena said in response to her questioning. "He was sitting at your pew. He didn't look happy. That's all."

The week after that, business began to pick up again, and so Amy wasn't at home for most of Tuesday. She definitely did not wonder what Al thought had happened to her. She definitely did not wear her earpiece around for extra long that day. She definitely did not want to see Al Borzoni again.

The birthmark seemed even more monstrous than it already had been in the weeks before she'd met Al. It seemed redder, puffier, and (if it was possible for skin markings to have emotional fits) angrier. It would not disappear beneath the foundation that she applied so liberally every morning. So she stopped using it. She even got up the courage to glare furiously at a whispering, giggling couple that she encountered on a subway that weekend as she and Lena rode it to the middle of the city where a farmer's market was taking place.

"The word is that there is all kinds of organic stuff being sold for really cheap," Lena had begged. "Cucumbers, melons, rhubarb...think of the pie you could make with that stuff."

"Don't tempt me," Amy had sighed. "I want pie so bad."

"Come with me, and we can make some tonight."

"I don't know."

"It's better than staying in and binge-watching MASH though, isn't it?"

"Binge-watching is a perfectly good coping mechanism."

"Not when you're guilt ridden and have had exactly zero downtime since spring started to roll around. Put your shoes on."

That had been that. Amy had changed her shirt, brushed her hair, and—yes—put on shoes. The ride was longer than what they usually took. Glaring and heated whispers aside, there was nothing remotely interesting about it. The car was filled with exhausted or hung-over men and women, and even Lena fell silent.

The farmer's market was one of the biggest that Amy had ever seen. Produce was piled up on the carts that had been wheeled out onto the stadium arena to protect from chilly weather. Men and women shouted from behind the stands, trying out catch phrases and words like 'environmentally friendly' to draw customers in. Children darted back and forth, giggling or screaming or passing out fliers for booths across the way. Lena collected four or five of those while they walked; Amy was heartily avoided by any and all children. She'd been told once that she looked like the Phantom of the Opera—which wasn't quite a good thing. Or so she had guessed.

"Isn't this great?" Lena asked, dodging through the crowd and pulling Amy along with her. "Look, here! Starfruit. Check this out!" She palmed a yellow and green fruit and shoved it at Amy. "Smell it. Taste the Carambola's delightful fragrance."

"Pay the guy first," Amy laughed as she held the fruit close and gave it a peremptory sniff as Lena fished a crumpled dollar bill from her pocket and slid it across the rough, makeshift counter.

They spent the next hour pushing through the ever-evolving crowd and sampling whatever they could. By the time morning turned into afternoon, Amy had a bulging bag of produce dangling from her shoulder. It was this traitorous bag that would prove to be her undoing.

It was almost twelve thirty when the bell rang to announce the beginning of the produce size and quality competition. Lena had—against Amy's better wishes, or so she liked to think—guided them into walking down the middle of the path. The crowd of wildly enthusiastic agriculture junkies hit without warning—disgruntled families, grumbly farmers, and pleasant landowners had formed an unstoppable mass. A mass that had no qualms about slamming, full-forcedly, into Amy's side and spinning her off to the side while Lena was swept along with it, towards the ever-important competition. In an attempt to steady herself—and protect herself from any further surprises—Amy grabbed hold of the plastic piping of a stand. She stood there, holding the pipe with one hand and gripping her bag with the other, and watched the wall of people snake past her. She was so focused that she did not notice a dark figure sidle up to stand beside her.

"It's amazing what the prospect of a spectator sport will do to a crowd of people," Al said, ignoring Amy's startled gasp. "And it's the strangest thing—smelling you rush by me in a crowded street, when I haven't seen you in weeks."

"You scared me," Amy said.

"So did you," Al shrugged. Even then—on a Saturday, in the middle of an agricultural event—he wore that gray suit. "Forgive and forget, that's my motto. Did you hurt yourself?"

"Wha—oh, no. I just got bumped around a little bit, and I lost my roommate in the crowd." Amy sighed. "I don't come out very often, you know. Something...like this always happens."

Al nodded and unfolded his aluminum cane. "I'll walk with you while you find her. If that's okay."

"That would be...great."

They waited for a moment, until they could be sure that the crowd was thinning, and then ventured out into the dusty roadway.

"If you don't mind me asking," Al said calmly as they passed a Mexican stand that offered mayonnaise covered corn on the cob, "Why haven't you been back?"

"To the church?" Amy adjusted the strap of her bag. "I just...I didn't feel like it would be a good idea."

"Church, or talking to me?"

"Not...definitely not you. Not you *at all*," Amy said. "You're great. But I'm not exactly a religious person..."

"Neither am I." Al shrugged.

"And I didn't feel like lying in a church was the greatest act of my life. So I decided to...not go back." Amy picked up the pace. "Sorry."

"Don't apologize," Al's cane clicked and clacked against the ground as they walked. "Never do that. Tell me what you lied about. Is your mouth really small? Are you taller than you told me?"

"It's stupid." Amy's step faltered. Her breath caught in her throat.

"It's not stupid if you don't think it is."

"Al..." She shook her head. "I know what I'm—"

"Amy." Al threw out a hand and collided with her shoulder. She stopped. "I like you. I feel like I would like you a lot more if you would just talk to me."

A crowd of children walked by, and Amy winced as she saw one, and then two, and then more heads turn to stare at her.

"Look at that," one said loudly. "That lady's a freak!"

"A witch, a witch," one chanted.

"No way that's her real *skin*!"

Amy winced again—at the exact moment that Al, with the speed of a bullet train, whipped around and slammed the point of his cane into the ground at the children's feet. "That," he growled, "Is not how you speak to another human being. Leave now."

They did—scattered like leaves on the wind, screeching in fear and abandon, and left Amy staring into the blank, angry eyes of Al Borzoni.

"I've got this birthmark," she blurted out. "It—it covers half my face and my...my neck. They're these big purple spots. Most of the time I try to cover it up, but people still can't stand it and I get things like *that* or I'm turned into some sort of charity case. I'm sorry, Al...I wanted to tell you what I looked like, but I wanted....I wanted..."

"You wanted me to see you as a person," he said in sudden realization. "But you never had to worry about that."

"I didn't know," she said. "I wanted you to see me as a whole person, not this..." her hand reached up to touch her neck. "Not this thing."

"But I knew about it," he said, and caught her wrist in his hand. "I always knew, from the minute I touched your face. The skin...the skin of your face is raised here—" he pressed the fingers of his other hand to her forehead. "Just a bit. I didn't ask because I knew it was something you weren't ready to tell, and I just wanted you to be comfortable with me, to talk to me so that we could get to know each other..."

"Oh, Al," Amy breathed. "I'm so sorry. I just...I didn't want you thinking I was someone I'm not, and I didn't know what to do."

"Well," he said. His hand slid up her wrist and found her fingers. "You don't have to worry anymore." He leaned forward. "I would like to kiss you now, Amy."

"Yes," Amy breathed. "I'd like that too."

She took his face in her hands and pulled him downward, even as she stood on her toes, to press their lips together. That, she thought, was what had been hiding in his smile the first day that they'd met in that cathedral. In that smile had been acceptance, kindness...everything that she had been looking for.

When the kiss did end, they walked around the fair hand in hand. The aluminum cane clicked and clacked along the ground as he told her about his extremely boring life as an accountant, and she laughed and countered with stories about her favorite customers at the travel agency. Every so often, he would stop and lift his free hand to touch her hair, or her nose, or her lips.

"Just right," he said. "Perfect Amy."

"Al," she would breathe, and then she'd turn and ask him what he wanted to see. She was good at that, he'd told her. She made him feel like he could see the sun rise and the earth turn and the stars sparkle up in the sky—all at the same time. That made her blush—and he felt her cheeks warm with the palm of his hand, even as she described a ramshackle collection of wheat sales booths. Afterwards, they went out for coffee and talked—and talked, and talked.

Until the sun rose on a perfect Sunday morning.

THE WINDOW BETWEEN US

CORA LAYNE

55

Chapter One

Loss

"I'm sorry, Claire. I just can't carry you anymore. I've made excuse after excuse to the school district in your defense. I'm sorry, but we have to let you go," Principal Hayes told Claire with a pained expression.

"Principal Hayes, how could you fire me at this point in my life?" Claire exclaimed tearfully, "My career is all I have left. I can do better, you know that."

"Claire, I'm going to tell you this as a friend—take this time to heal and get yourself back together. You are not the same since your divorce. I understand that this is a very difficult time for you. However, the students need the old Claire, not this Claire; you're constantly late, you've completely neglected the lesson plans required by the district and parents have reported about the inappropriate remarks you've made in the classroom. You didn't even show up to your own classroom's parent-conference day, for goodness sakes!"

"Do you want me to lie to them? Do you want me to tell them that life is all about rainbows and fairy tale endings?" Claire asked angrily.

"See, that is the kind of behavior that the district and I are concerned about. You are no longer fit to be in charge of these students and I will not tarnish my reputation with the school board for you! Please, you need help; focus on yourself right now, Claire. Give yourself a break. Your career will always be here but you are no good if you're behaving like a deranged woman!"

"You can't fire me for getting divorced! Where is your compassion? I've been a loyal employee of this district for ten years! You mean to tell me that nobody in this entire district has gone through what I'm going through?" Claire cried.

"You're clearly missing the point, my dear. You are being fired because your personal life has affected your performance as a teacher in this school and you are putting your students in jeopardy. Please, try to understand and be professional about this. If you'll excuse me, I have an appointment with a parent coming up shortly," he said coldly as he sat in his cushiony, leather office chair.

Claire knew he was not trying to be rude to her, after all, he'd always been kind to her in her years of employment there. While she knew that the principal had no ill intentions for firing her, she still felt betrayed. There was no point in fighting to keep her job; it was obvious that the decision had already been made and set in stone. She slowly got up from the chair across the principal's desk and said, "Well, I guess that's it then. I will have all of my belongings cleared out of my class by the end of the school day. Thank you for everything, Principal Hayes." He gave her a sad half-smile and held out his hand expecting a handshake, but Claire had already started towards the door.

On her way home, Claire thought about Principal Hayes' words about her. He was right, she was not the same. I could never be that Claire again. That Claire thought that Tim would always love her regardless of being infertile. She was naive and she was wrong because in the end—he left her. Claire had once heard from a psychologist friend of hers that when a person goes through a divorce, they go into mourning. Indeed, they do not experience the physical death of their spouse or their loved one, but they do experience the death of a future they dreamed of, worked for, and built along with their partner. Now, she felt like she had no future. She hadn't ever planned on being without him.

As she was driving, it occurred to her to pass by the drive-through of their favorite burger place. Every Tuesday, she would pick him up late after work and they'd eat in the car. They'd always share an order of French fries. So, she ordered herself a cheeseburger and an order of fries. She parked herself on the lot and ate her burger first. When she got to eating the French fries, she ate a couple then looked at the cardboard tray for a moment. She slowly returned the fry she had held up to her lips. It's too big to finish it all by myself. Claire began to sob uncontrollably. What little hope she felt. The one thing she had left had been snatched from her, too. Images flashed through her mind of future Tuesday's sitting in the car in this very lot, crying pathetically over her loss. Truly, it was impossible to imagine herself doing something else.

In the midst of her misery and self-pitying, her cell phone rang. She thought about letting it go straight to voice-mail but it was her father who was calling. Claire's father rarely called unless it was urgent, therefore, she wiped her face and composed herself.

"Hello. Dad?" she answered into the phone.

"Hello, Claire. Are you at work?" her father asked.

"No, I'm not. The last time you called me, it was to tell me that Ginger had swallowed a ping pong ball! I'm kind of worried about what it is this time," Claire chuckled.

"It's not about Ginger this time," her father replied before going completely quiet.

"Huh? Who is it about? Dad, are you okay? How's mom?" Claire was beginning to feel the dread creeping into her. She could hear her father taking deep breaths as if not to burst into tears.

"Dad, what is this about?"

"Your mother," he said, his voice breaking.

"What happened to my mom?" Claire asked desperately, "Has something happened to her?" Her eyes began to water as the worst possibilities started playing in her mind.

"Last night—your mother suffered a stroke. Today, the doctor has told me that your mother suffered some brain damage that might result in permanent paralysis. We won't know the exact extent of her brain damage until they can observe her while conscious. I'm afraid your mother is in a coma at this moment, Claire," her father managed to tell her in a trembling voice.

"Why didn't you call me as soon as it happened?" Claire asked sternly.

"I wanted to wait for the doctor's results. I didn't want to burden you if we didn't have to; I know that's what your mother would have told me. What, with all of what has happened in your life recently, I hesitated."

"I understand but that is my mother. I could be in a coma myself and I'd still want to know how she is!"

"I think it's time we close down our bakery, Claire," her father said sadly, "I'm going to have to take care of your mother full-time. There's no way I would pay for a caretaker to do it for me. I signed up for sickness and in health—taking care of her is my responsibility in these times." Claire got a knot in her throat as she listened to her father speak. *I can't even find someone to love me the way my dad loves my mom.*

"Dad, that's the only thing paying for your bills right now. What are you and mom going to live off of?"

"We will figure it out. We can move to a smaller apartment in a cheaper part of France or sell all of our belongings." Claire analyzed her situation during the conversation with her father and decided that it would be best if she moved back home to help with the family bakery. She realized right now would not be the best time to close down their only source of income given the circumstances. Her mother was going to need medical equipment, medications, and who knew what else. She wanted to help her parents the only way she knew.

"Let me come home to work at the family bakery," Claire proposed to her father.

"What about your job?" he asked concerned. She thought it best not to tell him that she had been fired to avoid causing more worries.

"I'll ask for a leave of absence or something. Don't worry, Dad, I can take the time off. It's really not a burden. I have to be near mom. You take care of mom and I'll run the bakery until she gets better."

Her father thanked her repeatedly for what she was willing to do to help her family. She had decided to leave the United States to fly across the world, back to her family's home in France. Claire started packing her belongings as soon as she got back to her apartment that night and she booked her flight for the following afternoon. The scare from the possibility of almost losing her mother made her forget about being fired. Claire's world was in shambles but she thought it'd be better if she actually helped her parents than cry pathetically in her car over too many fries. She had no suspicion that she was about to discover happiness in the very bakery where she grew up.

Chapter 2

Danish

Claire arrived in Colmar, France at nighttime. Her mother was in a different part of France in a larger hospital so she made a stop there first. Her father already had her keys to the house and bakery ready for her, as well as a list of duties to be fulfilled at the bakery. She had decided to hire a helping hand at the bakery that she would be paying out of her own pocket. Her father refused to take any money from her but she was persistent and finally convinced him.

"But they won't know the ways of our bakery," her father insisted.

"We will teach them. Dad, you forget I grew up in that bakery. I know it and love it as much as you do. Besides, without you there I am going to have my hands full. I'll make sure to let them know that it is only a temporary job until you and mom can get back," Claire argued.

"I guess you are right. It's just hard to trust someone else with our business. You know it has only been your mother and I working that bakery all these years."

"I know, Dad. But you trust me, right? It will be in good hands. You focus on mom and let me know if you guys need anything." She said her goodbyes to her father and to her mother, who was still unconscious and drove her rented car back to her parent's home.

When she entered her parents' home, she went straight to sleep as she was only getting a couple of hours of sleep before heading to the bakery in the morning to reopen. Claire felt a certain peace being in her parents' home in Colmar, thousands of miles away from Florida. It was almost like being able to relive her childhood and teenage years. She had left to America, met her ex-husband or been married. This is a good place to forget. Her former bedroom was long gone since her parents had it turned into a mini-library of sorts. She put her luggage down in the living room and slept on the couch.

The next morning, Claire woke before the sun rose. She quickly got herself ready and made her way to the bakery which was only down the street—less than a minute's walk. From outside of the bakery, she could see through the windows. The bakery appeared dark and empty. It looked more run-down than it did the last time she came to visit about 5 years ago. Once inside the bakery, she turned on the lights. She went to the back and turned on all of the equipment. It had been a while since she baked anything but, making pastries and sweets had been instilled in her since she was a child. She quickly began to mix her doughs and batters for all kinds of pastries and breakfast bread. The moment she started garnishing the pastries, it dawned on her that she was still quite skilled. The techniques came to her naturally.

A knock at the glass door startled her from her concentration. A glance at the round wall clock in the kitchen revealed that she had gone past 6 o'clock in the morning, which happened to be opening time for the bakery. She ran to the front of the store and looked out the door. It was a tall, light-skinned man with curly hair. His thin, dark glasses framed his hazel eyes. He wore blue jeans with an olive shirt and white sneakers. He waved and a smile revealed the slightest gap-tooth. Claire smiled back at him and quickly opened the door to let him in.

"Good morning," the man said, "am I rushing you? You didn't have to open because of me." Claire recognized his English accent.

"No, not at all. I was just in the kitchen baking," she replied.

"Well, this is a bakery," he laughed. Claire tried to go along with it but she was exhausted from the trip and from baking more than she'd done in ages.

She smiled and said, "What can I get for you today?" The man noticing her disinterest stopped smiling.

"I'll just have a blueberry Danish, please."

"Okay, I believe those are just cooling off on the kitchen rack. I'll be right back with your Danish," she told him politely. When she returned, the man smiled at her again.

"Thank you," he told her as he paid. As he was paying, he also pulled out a little card from his wallet and handed it to Claire. It was a miniature painting he had painted on the card. It appeared to be abstract flowers in a sunny field.

"What's this?" Claire asked holding up the card.

"It's a sunny field to brighten up your day," he said walking out the door.

Claire held the card in her hand and looked at it in puzzlement. At the same time, she was intrigued by the little thing. For the painting being on such a small surface as the canvas, it was extremely detailed. Claire was actually impressed. She taped the card to the wall behind the counter so that other customers could see the man's art. I hope I didn't come off as rude. Claire felt a tad bit guilty from the way she spoke to him. I hope he comes back so I can apologize. She got back to work; still thinking about the man she had been short with. Eventually, she forgot all about it when people started to enter the bakery for their baked goods. Closing time came around so, she cleaned the kitchen and all of the equipment. She was just finished sweeping and about to lock the front door when a young girl walked in. The girl couldn't have been older than 16 years old.

"Hello," the girl said faintly.

"Hi," Claire replied, "what can I get for you?"

"Actually," the young girl said, "I wanted to come in here to ask if there was any help wanted. I could really use the money."

"Why don't you ask your parents for an allowance? You shouldn't have to work. You should be focusing in school."

"That's the thing," the girl replied, "my father abandoned my mother and I not long ago. My mom works but we are struggling to make ends meet. We can't afford to buy my school books. I'm afraid my grades have already begun to suffer." Claire was overwhelmed with compassion for this young girl.

"What is your name?" Claire asked her.

"I'm sorry. I should have introduced myself first— I'm Alice."

"Okay, Alice. I'm Claire, by the way. I'm going to help you out. You have to be here every evening after school. You will help me prep for the next day and we will clean the equipment together. We receive shipments on Sunday mornings and you'll have to be her to help with those, too." Alice immediately began jumping up and down.

"Thank you," she exclaimed repeatedly, "thank you. When do I start?"

"Tomorrow is your first official day," Claire said as she walked behind the counter.

"You can count on me to be here," Alice said excitedly.

"Wait," Claire called out, "take this." She held out a substantial amount of money.

"Oh, I can't take that. That's too much," Alice told her pushing her hand back.

"Sweetie, consider it a hiring or sign-up bonus. Please, take it. I want you to buy your books tomorrow and anything else you might need to do well in school. I can trust you, right?"

"Yes, yes you can. I promise I will buy my books first thing in the morning. How can I ever repay you?"

"You're working for me now, aren't ya?"

"I sure am! Thank you, Miss Claire!"

"Go on home," Claire instructed her, "before your mother starts to worry."

"You got it, Miss Claire. Good night" Alice said as she closed the door leaving Claire alone in the bakery again. Claire finished her cleaning duties and closing routine before heading off to visit her mother in the hospital. As she was exiting the building, she looked at the painting behind the counter and smiled. She was so flustered that morning that she hadn't realized how handsome he was. What goofy gap-toothed smile. Without realizing it earlier, that man had made her entire day. Although, helping Alice made her day as well. The teacher in her would not allow her to not help a student in need of assistance. I failed my students back in America. The least I could do is help a child here at home. Claire recognized that she had been failing at being a role model and a loyal teacher in her last months at the school. It warmed her heart to realize that she still cared for students as a teacher does, whether it is a student from her classroom or not.

Chapter 3

Paintings

Over the next few weeks, the man became a regular customer at the bakery. Every morning, he was there at 6 o'clock ordering a blueberry Danish. Claire still had yet to ask for his name. He hadn't asked for her name so she was unsure about asking for his. One thing he never failed to do, however, was give Claire a new card with a painting for the wall behind the counter every time that he paid. Claire had begun to spend more time polishing herself in the morning EMDASH making sure that she looked out together. One morning the man even complimented her. She started to realize that the man would compliment her every time she wore a new piece of jewelry or had styled her hair differently. Claire decided that she was going to ask for his name the next time he came to the bakery. The thought made her nervous but she thought it was harmless. It's not like I'm asking him to date me. Even though, recently she had begun to imagine herself on dates with this man. I'm going to do it. I'm going to ask for his name.

The next morning, Claire had the man's blueberry Danish all ready for him to take. She placed it in the glass case besides the counter and waited for him to arrive. Alice was there on that particular weekday since it was a holiday and she had no school. She wanted to see what the bakery was like during her school hours. Alice took notice of Claire's appearance that particular day and was curious.

"You're looking dolled up today, Miss Claire," Alice complimented.

"Thank you, Alice. I had a couple of extra minutes this morning and decided to make myself more welcoming or pleasant looking," Claire said fixing her fringe that fell just above her eyes. The rest of her brunette hair was pulled into a high ponytail. Claire had also curled her eyelashes and applied a light pink blush to her ivory skin along with a mauve colored lipstick on her lips.

"That looks like more than a few extra minutes of polishing. Does Miss Claire have a crush?" Alice teased her à la high school mode.

"Are you finished decorating, silly girl? Get back to work," Claire said sternly. Alice made her way to the kitchen and Claire continued to wait. As always, the man arrived at the same hour, same minute as every other day.

"Good morning," he said to Claire as he walked to the counter.

"Hi," Claire replied, "how's your morning?"

"It's always a great morning for me," he said with a smile.

"I have your blueberry Danish ready for you here," Claire said as she took it out of the glass case.

"Wow, thank you."

He started taking out his wallet to pay for the pastry when Claire muttered, "So, I was wondering if—if you'd like to have breakfast with me here." She motioned towards a small café style table set at the corner of the bakery. The man stared at her unbelievingly. There was an awkward silence in the air and Claire had begun to worry.

The man flashed a smile and said, "Uh, I'm sorry I don't think I can. It's not a good time for me." Claire felt the sting of rejection.

"I'm sorry. I shouldn't have asked. Can we forget I asked? Okay, let me just package up your Danish," Claire said clearly hurt.

"Wait, I don't think you understood me," the man began, "I would definitely love to join you very much."

"Oh?" The man took out his wallet and paid for the pastry. He had a small painting for Claire, per usual, but instead of handing it to her, he placed it upside down and wrote something in the back of the card.

"I'm having an exhibit tonight. I'd love it if you'd come," he said as he finally handed the card to her. She looked behind the painting and his writing read: GALLAGHER'S GALERIE. 5 O'CLOCK. His name was also written on the card.

"Okay, I will see you at five—Abe. I'm Claire," Claire smiled.

Abe smiled on his way out the door. Alice appeared from the kitchen and said, "Ooh, Miss Claire's boyfriend is a cutie pie. Get it? Cutie pie. You know, because we work in a bakery."

Claire laughed, "He's not my boyfriend and I doubt he thinks of me that way."

"Well, I'm sorry I spied on you two for a little but I really think he likes you. He was giving you google-eyes as you counted his change and packed his Danish. You should have seen him."

"Did he really?" Claire asked hopefully.

"Uh-huh. What did he write on his painting?"

"It's the name of a gallery a few blocks from here. I'm pretty sure that he's an artist. He invited me to his exhibit tonight."

"Are you going?" Alice asked.

"I don't think I can. I'm usually not finished closing up by that time and I don't want to keep you here that late. It's too risky for you."

"Well, how about we clean up earlier than usual? I think you should give it a shot, Miss Claire. I think he really likes you."

"Alice, you're a child."

"And you are scared," Alice teased. After much persuasion, Alice convinced Claire to attend Abe's exhibit after work. Alice did extra chores in order for them to be able to close the store at four on the dot.

After the store had closed and Alice's mother had picked her up, Claire walked back to her parent's home to get dressed and touch-up her makeup. The thought of Abe gave her butterflies. She had not been on a date with a man, other than her ex-husband, for many years. She was hopeful, yet the dark cloud that had been hovering over her head since her ex-husband left would rain miserable thoughts on her. What if it's all great in the beginning until he finds out? What if he wants children? Claire felt so many fears holding her back. At one point, she even considered pretending to lose the card and not attending. She thought about her previously failed marriage and all the pain it had caused her. The pain she felt when she learned that her infertility was a deal-breaker for the man who had promised to love her in sickness and in health. What if he doesn't want kids, though? I should just be honest. Worst case scenario is he doesn't try to pursue a romance with me.

In the end, Claire decided to visit the exhibit. After all, Abe had always been friendly with her. She tried telling herself that she was only showing support to a good friend. Claire only took a few minutes to arrive at the gallery. There were a few people standing outside looking at the art pieces displayed near the windows. Claire peeked in and immediately concluded that the paintings inside the art gallery were the same style as the miniature paintings Abe had given to add to the bakery's collection. She made her way inside and soon after, Abe found her.

"Claire! I'm so glad you could make it," Abe said giving her a hug. He was dressed to impress in a gray suit and black tie. Claire had not ever seen him dressed so stylish until that point.

"Is this your gallery? I'm seriously impressed. I can't believe I never put two and two together. Of course, you're an artist," Claire said feeling dumb for missing that detail about him. He smiled at her, showing off his gap-tooth and she started to feel that nervousness again. She began to feel the fear of being hopeful and being let down in the end.

"It sure is. I had actually planned to invite you a few weeks back but you appeared to be extremely busy. I didn't want to bother you," Abe told her.

"I see. You were right! I'm only barely starting to get into a routine at the bakery. It's not easy running a business. I hope I didn't appear too unwelcoming but I apologize if I did."

"Oh, not at all. I understand; I was the same way when I first opened up this gallery a couple of months ago. You weren't unwelcoming at all. Truthfully, I was also scouting the place," Abe said.

"Scouting the place?" Claire asked suspiciously,

"Yes. I wanted to make sure your husband or boyfriend wouldn't appear out of somewhere and I'd get a beating for making a pass at a taken woman," Abe laughed. The words rung in Claire's ears.

"Why didn't you simply ask if I was taken?"

"I've kind of always been the shy guy. I spend a lot of time working on my art so I rarely get a chance to ask women out. I'm usually okay with that. But I have a feeling I would have regretted not asking you out," Abe said looking into her eyes. Claire thought that after her divorce it would be hard to ever trust the words coming out of a man's mouth but Abe spoke with such sincerity.

"Well, you finally asked me out," Claire said patting him on the shoulder. The two walked around the gallery talking about his paintings. Abe sounded like a true artist revealing what his inspirations were for each painting. They finally reached the main display. Claire's eyes grew wide and she drew in a gasp. It was a detailed painting of her father's bakery. Abe had painted every wrinkle on the wall, every chip in the paint, every miniscule detail of the bakery was in that painting.

"That's my parent's bakery," she said tearfully.

"Do you like it?" Abe asked.

"Do I like it? I love it. How were you able to capture the details so well?"

"I took a picture of it the day you opened late. Remember? That was the first time we met."

"I do remember. I felt so rude after you had left. I didn't think you'd come back," Claire told him shamefully.

"And I didn't know that I would be tempted to see your beautiful face every day."

"So, are you fairly new in Colmar?"

"I am. I'd only just arrived here the week prior to visiting your bakery. I've been working on a few of these paintings so I haven't had much time to explore." Claire took the chance to invite him on a tour of the city.

"Colmar is a beautiful place. I'm sure you don't need a tour to tell you that but would you like a tour of the city, anyways?"

"Are you asking me on a date?" Abe teased.

"I—," Claire blushed. This was an unusual experience for her. She was not accustomed to pursuing men, especially after her divorce.

"I'm just teasing you, Claire. I'd be honored to have you as my city tour guide," he grabbed her hand and he gave it a soft kiss. The rest of the evening was followed by Abe introducing his favorite baker, Claire, of course, to his friends that had come to visit from England. All of Abe's friends had wonderful stories to tell about him. It was obvious to Claire that he was very loved by many people. His demeanor and the way he carried himself was that of a true gentle spirit. He greeted everybody with a smile and took critique of his artwork with grace but did not allow the praises to inflate his ego. After going home that night, Claire went to bed with a smile on her face.

Chapter 4

Canals

On the Sunday that they had set for their tour of the city, Claire woke up early to meet Alice at the bakery for shipment. She was a little hesitant to leave Alice alone in her father's bakery but she had grown to trust the teenager for her displayed maturity and unfailing responsibility. She made sure to leave the glass cases full of baked goods for Alice and had also prepared a small gift for Abe, which she wrapped in a beautiful decorated box.

As Claire left the bakery she said, "I'm going to call you every once in a while to check on you but please call my cell if you need anything."

"Yes, ma'am! Don't worry, Miss Claire. I've got this under control. Have fun on your date with the painter!"

Claire and Abe had agreed to meet in front of his gallery a few blocks away. It was a few hours until lunch time so they had much time to explore. Claire stood in the front of the gallery waiting for her date to arrive. The windows were tinted quite dark so she was unable to see his paintings from the outside, which she lamented because they were breathtakingly beautiful.

"Claire!" Abe called from across the street. He waved at her and quickly ran across the street.

"Hello, Abe," Claire greeted him with a hug. Abe had presented her with vibrant yellow lilies.

"I have something for you, too," she added.

"A gift? For me? You shouldn't have," he said taking the box. He looked inside and removed a miniature blueberry Danish from it.

"Delicious, as always," he said as he bit into it. He took out another one and placed it in her hand.

"Sharing is caring," she said smiling. Abe laughed at her cute remark.

"I wanted to give you a miniature of something, you know, since you give me miniature paintings. Also, I'm running out of wall space, Abe!" she laughed.

"Thank you for this lovely gesture," he said gently shaking the box. "Where do we start?" he asked. They walked along the streets and admired all of the colorful homes and delightful storefronts. Claire suggested a couple of her favorite restaurants for their lunch later that day since he told her how curious he was about French cuisine. They passed by Claire's old high school and they shared hilarious stories about their high school experience. When lunchtime came around, they decided to rent a canoe and eat while traveling in the canals around the city.

"I'm so glad we did this," Claire told Abe, "It's been awhile since I've had fun." She stuck her hand out of the canoe and dragged it across the water. It was a beautiful, sunny day and the flowers that lined the canals were reflected in the water, making the water appear colorful.

"Thank you for showing me around. Colmar is a truly beautiful city—very charming."

"Do you plan on staying in Colmar?" Claire asked him.

"Should I plan on staying?" Abe asked. He looked at her intently and she knew he was being serious.

"I'm not sure what to say," Claire said looking away.

"I'd love to stay indefinitely if you accompany me on more outings like these."

"Abe, before this turns into anything, I have to tell you something." He nodded his head for her to continue. Claire went on to tell him about her life in America, her infertility leading to her divorce and about how she lost her job.

"I always told myself that if I ever met another man, I would tell him about my inability to bear children so he could decide whether he wants to stay with me or not," Claire finally said. Abe looked out at the water and remained quiet for a long time. Claire thought that maybe he was waiting for the canoe to reach the dock so he could just walk off and forget all about her. Tears filled her eyes but she pretended to look in another direction so he would not see her crying.

Abe cupped her chin with his hand and turned her face to his. He looked into her eyes and said, "I'm sorry to say, Claire, but your ex-husband is a fool." Claire wrinkled her forehead in confusion.

"The ability or inability to make babies does not and should not determine whether a person is loveable or not. It doesn't make a person worth more than the other of being with. You are not disposable, Claire. You are kindhearted and smart and funny and that man was lucky to have you. He's missed out big time," Abe told her. Claire was shocked by his reaction. She thought he'd react the same way her ex-husband had reacted—just completely devalue her as a person. *Why am I so surprised? Of course, he's not like my ex-husband. He's different.* Claire almost caused the canoe to tip over when she leaned in to wrap her arms around his neck.

"Thank you for your kind words, Abe," she said into his ear. Tears of joy still ran down her face. Abe pulled away and wiped the tears with the back of his hand. Claire felt the world around them become silent and blurry; only the two existed on that canal at that very moment. Abe leaned in and kissed her on the lips. The seconds that passed while their lips were locked felt like a frozen moment in time. Claire felt a connection she had never felt before, not even with her ex-husband. With that kiss, she gained a sense of belonging, and she knew right then that she was where and with she was supposed to be.

In the months that came, Claire's mother regained her ability to speak and was slowly regaining her body's mobility but was still unable to help at the bakery. Claire and her father took turns between caring for her mother and running the bakery. The bakery itself, was renovated and Abe's painting of the bakery's exterior hung in the entrance. Abe's card paintings were still on the wall behind the counter. Eventually, Claire was able to earn her teaching credentials in France and became a teacher at Alice's high school. Claire and Abe were married shortly after and ecstatic about adopting their first child. Sometimes, Claire thought about the night that she sobbed in her car at the burger place parking lot and thanked the universe for that rough time in her life—she would not have had the same deep appreciation she had for the new changes in her life.

TO TRUST AGAIN

NATASHA GROVER

To trust again...

When Annie's long-time boyfriend decides that the Amish way was no longer his way, she is left shattered, but worst of all single. She struggles to overcome rejection and prays for God to help her, but all she gets in return is silence. Barren and a spinster, she had lost all hope of finding love. But through revelation during a Sunday service, she discovers that there is hope, and that is when everything changes.

When Seth and his daughter Mary arrive in town, everything changes. A chance meeting with a beautiful woman who adores his daughter was nothing but the grand design of God.

God works in mysterious ways, and this is exactly what happens when two souls are meant for each other.

Chapter 1

Annie looked down at the small keepsake box Abel gave her last Christmas. She never thought she would feel this way, so deserted and lost. Abel was the only man she ever cared for and now he was gone, out of her life and out of her world, but still so very present in her mind. She couldn't believe it when he came to her just a month ago to tell her he was leaving for good. Everything seemed so perfect, she was happy; she thought he was happy and although he often told her how he would have liked to be able to study science instead of erecting barns and toil in the fields, she never expected him to follow that farfetched dream of his. After all, his father was the Bishop of Lititz and he knew the consequences of his actions, yet here she was staring eternity in its face with no hope to marry one day. *How could God have allowed this to happen*, she thought as tears welled up in her eyes, surely He would not have allowed such a worldly passion to overcome Abel and allow his servant and son to run into a world where evil is so rife.

"Annie, it's time to let it go," Anke said as she came to stand next to her.

"Not now Anke," Annie mumbled, wiping the tears from her cheeks.

"You've been a walking corpse since he left, you hardly eat and all you do is sit here and sulk, sooner or later the pain will go away, but only if you let it go."

"It's easy for you to say, you have everything," she blurted out and stormed into the house to find the solitude of her room.

Anke was her younger sister, what did she know of heartbreak? It wasn't as if she could simply turn off a switch and stop feeling so terrible. She was married, she had everything Annie ever wanted, she had a loving husband a child and her life was perfect. Anke knew better than to envy her sister, but her emotions were all over the place and right now not in the best of places either. If only she could turn back time and try harder to convince Abel to stay. But now that she had time to think things over it became more and more evident why Abel never proposed to marry her. He never intended to stay, and after Bishop King's passing, there was nothing to stop him from pursuing his dream. If he loved her like he so often said, then why did he break her heart? He didn't even ask her to join him, not that she would have, but if he had asked her then she would have been certain that he did in fact see a future with her, but then it would have been her choice to stay. But instead he went on his own, because he wanted to leave everything behind, including her.

She slammed the door to her room shut and pressed her back up against it, this raging sea of anger was suffocating her in ways unimaginable. She was angry with Abel, with Anke and even with her youngest sister Mabel. Convicted by the thought of being angry even with God, she tossed the keepsake box aside and fell to her knees.

"Forgive me Father; I'm a simple person with a broken heart. Please take away this pain and heartache," she prayed as tears streamed down her face, "Please help me to understand why everything is going wrong in my life. Have I not been a loyal servant?"

She waited expectantly for an answer or for the pain to miraculously disappear, but the silence was like a poison that seeped into her blood and paralyzed her. The emptiness she felt was overwhelming and cruel, "Why have Thou forsaken me?" she cried. It felt as if God had turned his back on her, even though she had no idea why. She searched the recesses of her mind, trying to make sense of it all, trying to remember any sins she may not have asked forgiveness for, but nothing came to mind. Rejected by her one true love and by God, she curled up on the floor and wept.

Chapter 2

Two days have passed, since her melt down in front of her sister, and thankfully Anke did not poke at her again, but the emptiness was far from gone. Numb she sat against the wall in Bishop Troyer's house with everyone else occupying the space for the Sunday Service. She felt almost alienated and the looks of sympathy she got from her peers didn't help her mood either, she was an utter disgrace, not to mention humiliating. All the other women her age was settled down with their own families. And at the age of twenty-nine she had nothing but broken dreams strewn in the wake of a failed relationship.

Caught up in her own thoughts she paid little attention to the service, until Bishop Troyer clapped his hands together and exclaimed loud enough for her to pay attention, "Trust in the Lord with all your heart and lean not on your own understanding; in all your ways submit to him, and he will make your paths straight."

That was her moment of realisation, all this time she had been trying to make sense of it all with her own understanding. And she was too emotional to thing rational, she still had a lot of questions as to why God had taken Abel from her when she was so sure they were promised to one day marry, but if she was going to get through all of this she was going to have to put her trust in God.

After the service she felt less burdened, almost as if a weight had been lifted, the longing was still there but it was lighter than before and instead of going home she took a walk down the small path that led to the a nearby brook. A time for reflection was nigh and by the grace of the Father, she could finally be free. She sat down in grass near the stream and closed her eyes, raising her face to the sun and soaking in it warmth. The spinning chaos that had altered her world over the past month or so was suddenly replaced by hope and for that she was grateful for.

"Daed!" a little voice called not far from where Annie was sitting and she quickly opened her eyes and looked up stream, and then she saw the little girl in her blue dress skipping towards her, and not far behind her, her father or so she would assume.

"Hello," the little girl said as she reached her, "why are you sitting here?"

"Mary, where are your manners?" her father reprimanded when he reached her, "I'm so sorry, she gets out of hand quite quickly," he apologised and Annie simply smiled.

"It's quite alright, I was just enjoying the fresh air," she said to the little girl, "My name is Annie," she smiled and extended her hand to the little girl, who suddenly shyly hid behind her father.

"She's embarrassed now," he chuckled and pulled her out from behind his legs, "Say hello to Annie."

"Hello Annie," the little girl, who couldn't have been older than five or six years greeted, with her thumb stuck in her mouth and her toes pointed to each other.

Annie did not recognize them, although their community was sizable and she didn't know a few people by name, she would surely have remembered the faces. And as far as she can recall she hadn't seen the little girl at the local school where she often helps out as a teacher's aid, but then she may not be six yet.

"I'm Seth," he said and tipped his hat, "Mary likes to come here whenever we come to Lititz."

So they were not from around here, she realized raising her hand to cover the bright sunlight streaming down from above, "Where are you from?"

"Rothsville, we came to attend the church service at least once a year in honour of my belated wife."

Annie's heart cramped in her chest, as she realized he was widowed, yet his tone of voice sounded uplifting as if he had made peace with his loss.

"Mamm died of cancer," little Mary piped up.

She had a maturity level Annie hadn't seen in a child for a long time, and realized that it may be because of her loss.

"My condolences to you," she cleared her throat, "It must be a difficult time for you."

"It's been a year and some months now, Meryl was from here originally, and I promised her that I will bring Mary here, she always liked it here by the stream."

"Why do you come here?" Mary asked again and this time Annie pushed herself up to on to her feet.

"Well I like the stream too, especially the flowers that grow on the banks," she smiled and ironed down the front of her dress, "But I'm done now, so you can play here as long as you want."

"Oh no, you don't have to leave," Seth objected.

Annie smiled at him and shook her head, "I have to get going anyway, and I only came here for a little while to clear my head."

"Why don't you stay?" Mary pleaded and tugged on her hand.

Annie's heart warmed to the little girl, she was adorable. With big blue eyes and blonde curly hair that stuck out from under her bonnet. She was sure that Mary was Seth's ray of sunshine.

"Maybe next time, I have to go and prepare food with my sisters."

"Let go of Annie's hand Mary," Seth instructed his daughter and pried her away, "I'm sure we will meet each other again and then you can invite Mary to join you here at the stream."

"What a lovely idea," she smiled, "maybe I will pack a few eats for the next time you come here."

Little Mary nodded excitedly and Seth simply smiled at her, which caused her tummy to tumble. He was a handsome man, and probably not much older than her. Not to mention his lovely little girl.

"I will see you around some time," Annie said and then waved as she headed up the small path.

What a chance meeting, she thought. Here she was down and out and God had just revealed to her that He is still in control, and then she meets this charming little family, who despite their loss, can still smile and radiate such hope and passion that it could ignite a fire. Just to see them together warmed her heart. She looked back again and smiled as little Mary waved back at her.

Chapter 3

Seth looked at Mary where she played on the edge of the stream, floating leaves like little boats downstream. Every now and again she placed a pebble on one of the bigger leaves and when it didn't sink she squealed excitedly. She reminded him so much of Meryl, her summer blonde hair that curled like her mothers' and the dimples that indented on her cheeks when she smiled. It's been over a year since his wife had passed away from cancer, and although he accepted it a long time ago, he's only now starting to feel human again now. He had been on autopilot since her death, having had to focus on Mary and raising her, in a way he was grateful that he had his little girl. Having someone to depend on him during such a difficult time eased the hurt and pain somewhat. That was the way of life, the weak always cares for the weak, it is how God intended it. He just wishes he could have been able to save Meryl, then she could still be here watching Mary grow up.

He lay back in the grass, hitched up on one arm, He dared not question God, he knew that through the storm, God had a plan and he was going to wait on God to reveal that plan no matter how long it takes.

His thoughts shifted to the woman he had met earlier, she wasn't young enough to be unwed, and she wasn't a widow, but yet she is unattached, which he found strange. A woman with such a beautiful smile would have many possible suitors.

"Seth!" a distant voice drew him out of his reverie.

He looked up and noticed William headed his way. William was one of his friends who lived here, and whenever he came to visit, he stayed with him. He raised his hand and waved, still keeping a vigilant eye on Mary.

"Finding you is no easy task," William said as he reached him.

"You know I bring Mary here right after church whenever I'm in town," Seth said and chuckled as Mary jumped up and down to cheer on her fleet of leaves.

"She's grown up since I last saw her."

"Yes she has, but we haven't been here for some time."

"True," William nodded, "I actually came to ask if you would be up to help us out with a barn rising. Our planner, well he upped and left unexpectedly and we need someone with skill to draw up the plans."

A barn raising, it's been years since Seth had taken part in any of those, the last time he did was over three years prior to his wife's passing. He had to admit, the thought of staying here while longer was tempting. Mary will get to come here every day, he would be able to put his skills to the test, and maybe, just maybe he will be able to get to meet Annie again. That thought crept in there without warning and he quickly cleared his throat and mentally shook his head. There was no time in his life for romance; he had a daughter to care for and a business to run. As a carpenter he prided himself in the work he could do, simple yet sophisticated pieces of furniture, sold not only to the Amish community but also to outsiders who valued solid oak furniture. And with the off cuts he made small ornaments and bird houses which he sold at a local stand just outside Rothsville.

"So what happened to the other chap?" he asked curiously.

"He got tired of our ways and headed out into the world."

"That's a pity, but I guess I can hang around a little longer if you don't mind that Mary and I stay on at your place."

"Of course I won't mind, you're always welcome here you know that."

The sudden jolt of excitement made Seth grin from ear to ear. It looks like this year was a year of the Lord's favour; he will finally get to work on something significant again.

He called for Mary and she quickly came skipping towards him, she was going to be so happy to stay here, he just knew it.

"How would you like to stay here for a few weeks?" he said as he knelt down on one knee, while dusting off dry leaves and grass from her dress.

Her infectious smile spread across her face and her eyes lit up, "Really *Daed*?" she said with her child like enthusiasm, "Will I get to see Annie?"

Taken by surprise that she actually mentioned Annie, he cast a quick glance to William, who stood with his arms crossed and an amused expression on his face.

"She was here at the brook when we got here, Annie likes her," he fibbed for an excuse.

"Sure she does," William smirked.

"Can I daed, can I?" she pleaded as she hopped unto his one knee.

"I'm sure we can make a plan," he said, how could anyone say no to such a face.

As the three of them headed back up the small hill towards civilization, Seth couldn't help but think about Annie, the friendly yet mysterious woman with the radiating smile, who seemed to have captured his daughter's attention. She had never taken to any other woman like this before, not even Grace, Meryl's younger sister.

"A penny for your thoughts," William said and grinned at him.

Seth chuckled and hooked his thumbs into his suspenders, he might as well be out with it, "It's been more than a year since Meryl passed away, sooner or later Mary will need a woman to teach her how to conduct herself appropriately. Teach her how to quilt and bake bread and so on."

"And you're thinking of Annie?" Willian asked as he kicked a stone out of the way.

"Not specifically, but meeting her and seeing how much Mary enjoyed her company made me think about it."

Who was he kidding, of course he was thinking of Annie. He met some other women from his own town who were all too willing to step up and fill Meryl's shoes but he never really paid any attention to their advances. But now out of the blue, all he could seem to think of was her.

She was heaven sent, no doubt and if he didn't at least try, he would never know.

"Ay, well, Annie has had her heart broken and she's been a difficult one to get on with ever since, so good luck."

"Did it happen recently?" he asked curiously.

"About a month ago, you know the planner I told you about? Abel was his name. He just came out one day, said his good byes and left. I believe he went to New York to study science."

"And left her behind too..."

Seth felt a great deal of sympathy for her, and his heart ached. He could only imagine how much pain she must have gone through when that happened. It's one thing to send someone off to the beyond, but having someone leave out of free will to explore the world out there was like a slap in the face.

"Yeah, it was rather sad, they looked happy together."

"Clearly he was not happy, otherwise he would not have broken her heart," Seth defended.

He knew that he was going to have to take one step at a time with Annie, and not push her into anything she didn't want. But if there was one thing he would do for her, whether they ended up together or not, was to show her that God has a plan for all his children.

Chapter 4

The quietness of the early morning was peaceful, there were no birds singing their morning songs or a rooster crowing to announce the start of a new day and the sun was still buried behind the horizon. Annie closed her eyes again as the heady pull of her dreams beckoned her back to play, but she had to wake up. There was too much to do on this blessed day. The past month she spent wallowing in self-pity had robbed her of some precious time such as baking bread and taking it to the local store, not to mention her chocolate cookies everyone always used to love so much. And maybe if she was lucky, she may be able to get some of those cookies to Mary before she departed with her father.

Even for an overcast day, nothing could dispel the mood Annie was in, for the first time in weeks, she felt alive again and ready to take on the world.

"You're up early," Eva said as she entered the kitchen, "and you're baking?"

Annie smiled at her youngest sister and nodded, "Yes, it's time I stop fussing over Abel and get on with life."

Eva ran around the table and threw her arms around her neck, "Thank goodness! We were all getting so worried about you. I'm so glad you've come to your senses."

Annie laughed and hugged her sister back, it's only now that she realized just how much she inconvenienced everyone around her and she was relieved that it had all come to an end. Yes, she may still think of Abel from time to time, but it no longer affected her as it did just a day ago before God had spoken to her heart. And if she can embrace the change with a positive attitude, then she will only be blessed richly.

"I'm sorry I had you all so worried, but it's all in the past now," she said as tears sprung to her eyes.

"No need to apologize, you and Abel were together for a very long time."

Eva released her and reached for one of the cookies on the cooling rack, and then picked up her quilt basket, "I have to go, but when I get back I want to hear how on earth this paradigm shift took place."

"Of course," Annie laughed and swatted her sister's hand away, "These are for Mary, and I'll bake another batch for the house later this afternoon."

"Who's Mary? Oh wait, don't tell me, I'm going to be late, but when I get back later you can tell me everything."

And like a whirlwind Eva left the house.

Later than morning after delivering the baked flat breads to the local store Annie's mood had taken a turn for the worst, but not because of Abel. She had hoped to see Mary and Seth but it seemed that she was too later. The realization that they had left to go back to Rothsville left her empty. She should have asked them when they were leaving instead of putting in all the effort to bake cookies for Mary. A soft sigh escaped her lips as she made her way towards Anke's house, at least the cookies will be put to good use there, she thought.

"Mary!" A little voice called out to her and Anke's heart leapt with joy and she spun around.

"There you are," she smiled, "I thought you had gone back home."

"Oh no, daed said that we'll be staying here while he builds a barn," she exclaimed and hugged Annie's leg.

"She beat me to it," Seth said when he reached them.

Annie's heart fluttered in her chest and she smiled up at him, next to him the top of her head only reached his shoulder. She was just as excited as the toddler clinging to her dress having learned that they will be staying on for a while. Normally Abel would be the one drawing up the plans for the barn and making sure everything was in order. It used to be so exciting watching him loose himself I the work.

"Where will you be staying?"

"We'll be staying with William and his wife; he was kind enough to open his door for us."

"That's good yah," and she went down on her knees to get to Mary's level, "I baked you some chocolate cookies," she said holding out the small tin.

Mary beamed and immediately took the tin from Annie and dug in.

"Thank you Annie," Seth said as she stood up, "Mary has really taken to you."

"She's a lovely child."

For a moment, Annie was lost in Seth's gaze and his smile that could make the world around her fade into the background. Mary had his smile with his dimples as well as his sky blue almond shaped eyes, there was no doubt that she was his daughter. The only difference was that he had he had brown hair. His wife must have been a beautiful woman, she thought briefly before little hands drew her attention again.

"Daed said that I can stay here today while he goes to fetch our clothes, only if I stay with you."

She was so caught up in her own thoughts she never heard that part of the conversation, and the toothy grin Mary gave her arrested her.

"Well, if you don't mind leaving her with a complete stranger, then I'm happy to take care of her for you," she smiled.

"You're not a complete stranger and William did say you were good with children."

So she had been a topic of discussion between him and William? Now more than ever, she was intrigued by Seth. But if she had been the topic of discussion hen surely William had divulged the bit of information about Abel.

"Of course!" she said out loud, "You're here to take over what Abel failed to complete," she blurted out unceremoniously.

"Pardon me?"

"Abel, he used to do the plans for the barns,"

"Oh yes, Abel. That's right. William asked me to help out."

A small frown creased on his forehead and Annie almost kicked herself, that wasn't even the conversation topic. The whole thing was about her taking care of Mary.

"I'll watch Mary for you," she railed back on to the topic, "we're going to have a lot of fun."

"Will you make my hair like yours?" Mary asked and Seth laughed.

"Like mine? But what is wrong with your hair, it looks beautiful."

"It's too curly and dead can never brush it."

She looked back at Seth and he shrugged, "It's always tangled, you have no idea how difficult it is to brush her hair."

"Well I have just the solution for your problem," Annie said grinning.

The poor father had no idea how to raise a daughter, and if she could help in any way she was more than happy to.

Chapter 5

Barn raising day...

It was a fine summer's day, and the weather couldn't be more perfect. The entire community had gathered to do the barn rising for the Yoder family, who had lost their barn in a fire two months ago, and while the women were all busy making food and helping with odds and ends, the men got ready for a hard day of teamwork.

Seth stood at the table at the far side of the grounds looking over his plans again. Although raising a barn was a much bigger project that putting together tables and chairs he was confident that I was flawless.

"So word has it that you're keen on Anny," William said as he came to stand beside him.

"Is that so?" Seth chuckled.

"Yah, yah, I've heard the talk in the town. Her sister Anke actually asked me outright if I knew anything."

Seth crossed his arms over his chest and glanced towards the tables where the women were gathered. There among them all sat Annie with Mary in deep conversation. He had only been here for two weeks, and during this time he had grown fond of her. But there was always the question that poked at his conscience. Was he attracted to her simply because she got on so well with Mary, or was he attracted to her because she was, well, Annie.

"She's a pretty woman, and she's very good with children," Seth admitted, trying not to say too much.

"Come on Seth, it's more than that. She's good with children yah, but she will make a fine wife. You should go on and talk to her."

"I'm sure she does, but I don't know if she is over Abel at all."

That was a truth he could not deny. She had hardly spoken about Abel during their meets at the creek, but the way she reacted that morning when she realized that he had taken the work Abel was meant to do, indicated that he still affected her. And how would he compete with that?

"Trust me, according to Anke, her entire mood changed since the day you arrived, she just needed a shove in the right direction."

"Well at least I accomplished something," Seth joked and elbowed William, "We can jabber on about her later, right now we have a barn to finish. Are the men ready to start?"

William shook his head and chuckled, "They are all ready, but if God wills for you two to get together, you know that no power on earth or in heaven can prevent that, right?"

"Then we shall see what God has in store."

William was right about one thing, if God had his hand in this and the only reason he ended up in this community was to meet Annie, then he prayed that God's will would reign over his fleshly emotions that have been running rampant of late. If not, then he will finish this barn here today, and return to Rothsville a sane but proud father.

By the end of the day the structure stood high against the afterglow of the setting sun, and families were slowly making their way home. Seth was pleased by the work that was accomplished in one day and the fact that he was able to lay out the plans to such perfection made him proud to say the least. With only the Yoder's left along with the odd family friends, Seth made his way to where Mary was helping Annie pack away the excess food. For a moment he looked at the two of them and couldn't help but smile. Annie really did like Mary, and if he had to be honest with himself, he liked her too. She was a beautiful woman with a heart of gold and a soft spot for Mary.

Chapter 6

The barn had finally been completed, and Annie knew all too well that soon she would have to say her farewells to Seth and Mary, and that thought alone left a lump in her throat. She really liked them, especially Mary. Annie swallowed at the lump in her throat; she would never be able to have her own children, not since the unfortunately surgery when she was only twenty that left her barren. And having been able to spend these few weeks with Mary really left her wishing for a miracle.

"You should tell him how you feel," Eva said at the breakfast table.

"You mean Seth?" Annie said blushing slightly.

Eva laughed and reached for Annie's hand, "Everyone can see that you two like each other. He's a widow and you're a spinster, you're simply perfect for each other."

"I would never be so forward!" Annie exclaimed laughing, "If he feels the way everyone assume he feels, then he would have to do the ground work."

Eva raised a brow, "And if he doesn't because he is to shy?"

"Then so be it, but I am not going to embarrass myself, what if everyone is wrong about him?"

"Trust me, we're not wrong."

Eva was persistent, for one she was young and full of happily ever after dreams; secondly, she was a self-proclaimed match maker. But even if Eva was right, Annie simply refused to put herself in the firing line. It would be up to God to guide her way, not her own understanding. Her own understanding when it came to Abel didn't help one bit, so she was going to have to simply put her trust in God and hope for the best outcome.

A slight knock on the door drew the sisters' attention and Eva was the first to rush to open the door and a few seconds later, it was Seth and Mary standing in their kitchen.

"Why don't you two join us for breakfast," Eva invited.

"Oh no, we've already had breakfast," Seth said, never taking his eyes of Annie.

Eva's gaze moved from Seth to Annie and back to Seth, when she raised both brows and fought to hide a smile.

"Mary, come with me, I want to show you my room."

Relieved Annie let out breathless sigh and stood up.

"I suppose you would have to go back to your home now that the Barn is up?"

The way Seth stood shifting his weight from one foot to the other, with his head in his hand made her smile, he looked so nervous. If only he could hear the frantic beating of her own heart.

"Yah, I have to go back. I have a business to run which I have neglected while staying here," he said and looked around the kitchen.

"I'm sorry," Annie said and cleared her throat, "I'm confident that God will help you make up time for your generous act of kindness to help the Yoder's."

Without warning, Seth stepped forward and came around the table until he stood in front of her. Of course her heart stopped and the zooming bees in her stomach did not help her one bit.

"Thank you for helping out with Mary," he said with his eyes downcast.

"That was no problem at all; maybe when you come back, I can help again."

She meant it, every word. She would do anything to spend some more time with Mary and teach her how to bake and quilt. The way she felt now, she wished that this would never end. But what she wished for more was for Seth to tell her how he felt.

"I've actually been thinking," he started and Annie held her breath.

"Yes?"

"Well, you get on so well with Mary, and well, we get on well too..." he paused and shuffled closer, "I know I'm not going about this the right way, but I was thinking or rather wondering if you would like to come with us to Rothsville."

Annie's mouth fell open and she stared at him, "You mean move there?

Seth nodded and shrugged, "We've only known each other for a short while, but when Jacob saw Rachel for the first time, he wanted to marry her right away..."

It felt as if Annie's entire world was turned on its axis and spinning in the opposite direction, did Seth just ask her to marry her or was she misunderstanding the meaning behind his words?

"What exactly are you proposing?" she said in a trembling voice.

"Oh for heaven's sake! He's asking if you'll marry him!" Eva shouted from the passageway.

Just then Mary came running out flinging her arms around Annie's legs.

Seth shrugged and smiled, "In short, yes. I mean I will go the Bishop first to ask for his blessing, but I have grown very fond of you and so has Mary, and after the time we spent together, I've come to realize that God had brought us to this place."

Her eyes shot full of tears and Eva lifted Mary up in her arms, twirling around and cheering, while her and Seth simply looked at each other.

A simple yes was all it took and Annie's dreams had come true. She found love in the strangest of circumstances and when she least expected too. On top of that, she would get to teach Mary everything that is good.

~*~

Seth could hardly have believed it was it not for the fact that he pinched himself for the umpteenth time. But there she stood, in her wedding garments. As beautiful as the first day he saw her near the brook and she was finally going to be his. But he knew that it was only by the hand of God that he had finally found a woman who will be good to both him and his daughter. And that was Annie, beautiful sweet spinster, Annie.

FOR A FIREFIGHTER'S HEART

MARISA MEYER

Chapter 1

Christine Rossouw assessed the destruction left behind by the blaze that reduced the Mulders' house to nothing but a pile of rubble and ash. It was pure luck that no one had gotten hurt in the blaze. The fire had started in the early hours of the morning when the Mulders' were still fast asleep. Now they all stood on the sidewalk, with nothing but the clothes on their back and their pet cat Malfoy, looking in horror at what was left of their home. Their belongings and their memories had literally gone up in flames. Now that was something she could never fathom, why would a family who lived day to day, turning over every penny have to endure such hardships? Why could this not happen to someone who could afford it?

It's the Lord's way to test our faith; her father's voice reminded her. To her it was more an excuse used by churchgoers to explain away logic, and logic told her a long time ago, that man's path is not destined or designed by God, but that man's path is a series of truth or dares onramps to new beginnings and disastrous endings.

She ducked under the warning tape that stretched across the front lawn, here and there, there were a few firefighters ambling around, just to ensure that the fire had been completely snuffed. Her job was to investigate the cause of the fire and fill our mounds of paperwork for insurance claims. She stepped over what used to be the threshold of the house, into what was left of it. Everything was charred black, logically, if the Mulders had all been asleep, and still managed to get down the stairs and out the front door, the fire could only have started at the back of the house or possibly the basement. Instinctively she traipsed over the rubble making her way through to the back of the house where the Laundry area used to be.

It took her close to an hour to determine the area where the blaze started and another hour to determine if it was accidental or not. In no time she had drawn the conclusion that the fire started as an electrical short in the laundry area. Apparently, Mrs. Mulder often left her tumble dryer on overnight. This, of course, would make claiming insurance a little more troublesome. Yet another flaw in the system, the insurance company is going to find every reason not to pay out the claim, by basing it on negligence, no wonder people were so up in arms with short term insurance places.

When she finally walked into her office by noon, she was finished, it's been one of those days where you barely get time to drink a cup of coffee, much less have lunch. The thought of lunch made her tummy rumble and she turned left down the hall to where the company's cafeteria was. She never ate here, but today was an exception. She had been up since 4 AM after being called out by the Fire Chief, and right now a greasy Burrito even sounded like heaven.

When she got back to her desk, there was a note that read – *Love me tender love me true, why not date me until you're blue.*

"Okay, guys! Who did it?" she asked as she crumpled up the note and dumped it in the trash.

None of them owned up but all of them laughed behind their sleeves. She knew that they all thought she was the odd one out, not being interested in dating and all. Whenever there was a company function that allowed partners, she went alone. If they all went out to drinks, she went alone. Now, it wasn't because she was anti the whole prospect of dating; it was just that she had no interest in getting tied down to one person who eventually ends up changing your character.

She had seen it so often. People lose their individuality, they change, and not for the better either, and years down the line, one or the other regret the fact that they had changed, and that's when trouble spoils paradise. Obviously, her current outlook on life came at a price. Just out of college, she dated Darryl, who was a very responsible young man with high ideals and in her opinion far-fetched dreams, but he was nice. In the beginning, like every other relationship, they both had different interests, but they both tried to get involved, she went with him to Nascar races, and he went with her to theater performances.

Then they started to get comfortable and suddenly she was going to all the car races, and he came up with every excuse under the sun not to go to a theater. But it got worse, slowly but surely he started to get his back up whenever she went to the theater alone and then they ended up fighting more than anything. It was there when she finally pulled the plug on their relationship and promised herself never to date again, against her mother and fathers' wishes of course.

The ringing of her phone, drew her out of her train of thought and she reached for the receiver, "Rossouw speaking," she answered absentmindedly while she shuffled through the stack of paperwork on her desk.

"Oh, hey dad," she said and pinched the received between her shoulder and her ear. "Mmm no, I haven't forgotten... yeah... mmm... well, I'm kind of busy... I know, I said I would be there but something came up... seriously, dad, it's not like the church is going to run away... Okay fine, I'll be there... yeah, I love you too."

She pulled out the incident report from one of the arson cases she had to submit to the lawyer and shoved it into the out basket, then dropped her head on her arms. She loved her parents, but her dad was forever begging her to go to church. Another place she tries to avoid at all cost. Church people were probably the most hypocritical beings alive, she thought despondently, but she knew that if she went to this one service, they would leave her alone for several months before they begged her to visit again. So she was going to simply suck it up, go, and get it over and done with.

Chapter 2

Jarod looked at himself in the mirror as he fixed his tie, it was still a while before the church would start, but he preferred to be the first one in and the first one out, usually picking the last pew right in the corner. He had a very trying time after his divorce, nearly lost his job and everything he had, because of it. Was it not for Pastor Rossouw who helped him to see the light, he would still be staring at the bottom of the bottle. He was never much of a drinker during his marriage, but after he found out that Elaine cheated on him, he drowned his sorrows, the only way he knew how. It's been two years since they went their separate ways and it was just like Pastor Rossouw had said, his hatred had turned to indifference, and the love he once felt for Elaine had subsided. He often saw her in town, but there was no more anger or bitterness. The point is that they were two different people, and in the end, they simply drifted apart. Elaine wanted kids and a house with a white picket fence, two dogs, and an SUV, with a husband that worked nine to five. He couldn't give her that, not at the time anyway. So, as a result, she went out and found what she wanted. He was happy for her, he truly was, but he promised himself that he would never marry again and committed himself to the fact that he would focus on work and God.

"Morning Jarod," Pastor Rossouw greeted as he unlocked the church.

"Morning Pastor, lovely day today, isn't it?"

"Indeed, we need the rain; hopefully it's here to stay for a few days."

The unexpected gift of rain had been a blessing after weeks of drought and unbearable heat, and although the rainy season was still a few weeks ago, the skies didn't lie. Jarod loved the rain.

"According to the weather, we can expect rainfall for at least three days," he chuckled and then entered the church and waited for the pastor to turn the lights on.

"Are you going to move up a pew?" Pastor Rossouw asked.

Jarod shook his head and smiled, "Maybe next time."

The pastor didn't push him, but he always asked him out of interest more than anything, that was the extent of their conversations. More small talk really. The pastor went on about his business and Jarod took a seat in his usual spot, waiting patiently for the pews to fill up.

Today, however, with the rain falling, he didn't expect the church to be packed. He always found it rather odd how people would run about in the rain to get to Walmart or go places, but the moment it rains they use it as an excuse to skip church.

One by one individual and families arrived, filling the pews from the front of the church towards the back. Two youngsters came bolting down the side aisle and darted between a couple talking in the front, then they disappeared under the pews. No one seemed to be perturbed by their playfulness, which he liked. Then again the sign right above the small stage read – Let the little children come to me, and do not hinder them.

He turned his attention back to the small hymnal in his hands, and paged aimlessly through it, trying to appear preoccupied, in the hope that no-one tried to make any conversation with him. But his hopes were dashed with Pastor Rossouw spoke next to him.

"Jarod, I would like you to meet Christine, my daughter."

Jarod stood up and wiped his hand on the back of his jeans and then extended it to the woman in front of him. She was beautiful, tall with long blond hair that flowed loosely over her shoulders. But the smile that tugged at the corner of her lips didn't reach her light blue eyes. It was as if the lights were on but nobody was home, she was just going through the motions.

"It's a pleasure to meet you, Christine," he said and shook her hand firmly.

"It's a pleasure," she repeated his words and removed her hand.

"Jarod is a firefighter, I thought you two would have a lot in common," Pastor Rossouw piped up and Jarod wanted to shrink away, but he remained poised.

"You're also in the department?" he asked out of interest.

"Not exactly, I'm in forensics, I investigate the aftermath and the cause of the fire," she answered.

"Nice," he said, not sure what else to add.

He felt awkward with her, not in a negative kind of way, but purely because he hasn't spoken to a woman on a casual basis since before he was married. And when the pastor walked away leaving the two of them alone in each other's company, he shrugged and stepped back.

"You can sit here if you want?" he offered.

This time she smiled, "I won't mind at all, anything but sitting right in the front where my dad wants me."

Jarod chuckled and moved over two spaces, leaving enough space between them. They sat in silence for a while before Christine spoke.

"You have to excuse my dad, he can be very forward at times," she smiled, "He keeps wanting to set me up for dates."

Jarod laughed at that, "Playing pastor and matchmaker, I see."

She rolled her eyes, "Yeah, he does it every time I set foot in a church, which is why I'm never here," she turned to look at him, "I haven't seen you here before, though."

He shrugged, "I've been here a few months now, but I don't stay around to mingle with the members. I just come for my daily bread and then I disappear."

"Ah, I see," she said, "The dash and go type."

"Yeah, that would be me."

"You do know that church is meant for communion and encouragement from fellow Christians."

He leaned forward with his elbows on his knees and regarded the congregation, "I come here to learn and find peace."

"A man with depth, well I'm sure you'll find peace being stuck here in the back all the time."

"It's worked so far."

Throughout the service, Jarod was acutely aware of the woman who was seated next to him. The aroma of her perfume kept wafting past him, making him shift uncomfortably in his seat. By the time the service came to an end, he couldn't wait to get out. He needed fresh air and fast.

"Well Jarod, it was a nice having company here at the back," Christine said as she stood up to let him pass.

"Yeah, it was," he dragged his hand over his stubbly short hair, "I'll see you around?"

All she did was nod, and that was his queue. He exited this church like a bolt of lightning.

Chapter 3

Christine did not expect that at all. She knew her father was up to something when he insisted on her coming to church. She was prepared for the worst, him introducing her to another pastor, or one of the deacons, or worst case, preaching hellfire and brimstone to try and get her to get back into the habit of going to church. The last thing she expected was to be introduced to a firefighter. And not just any firefighter, Jarod Marks had all the bits and pieces that would make any woman turn into a fan-girl. He was built like an MMA fighter, he had deep willow green eyes and brown, almost black hair that was neatly trimmed and on top of that, he had that five o'clock shadow that danced across his chin, making him look even manlier than he possibly could. For the first time in years, she wondered if her anti-dating motto was even viable. Just because she made one bad choice in life, by dating Darryl, didn't mean that every man she met would be like him.

After the service, she had spoken to her dad and tried to find out more about Jarod, of course, her dad was all too happy to tell her that he's a firefighter, with a deep soul, but beyond that, he didn't want to divulge any personal information. He did, however, mention that Jarod had also been in a bad relationship that left him weary of dating, much like her.

So what if he was damaged goods, she, though, he couldn't possibly be more damaged than she was.

Thankfully thinking about Jarod and the possibility of entering the dating scene again was a momentarily lapse in judgment, but the next day, she had once again gotten her mind focused on work and making sure she didn't fall into the dating trap again. Or so she thought. Every now and again, when she wasn't going through case files or looking at labs of fire starters that contained possible chemicals, Jarod's face floated into her mind. It got to a point where she went for her second visit to the cafeteria in one week, which was totally out of character. This time she opted for a slice of cheesecake and strong coffee.

"Rossouw!" one of her colleagues called. "Having a love affair with that cheesecake?"

"Shut it, Kemp," she mumbled and took a generous scoop out of spite and shoved it all into her mouth.

Dalton Kemp came over and pulled the chair out, plonking himself down, "You really need to get out more, we're having a get-together tonight at Franks' are you coming around?"

Franks was a bar not too far from the office, where they staff often went to wind down after a rough day at the office. Most of the time she opted out of going to mingle, but tonight was an exception, she needed a distraction.

"Yeah sure, I'll see you there at around seven."

"Great, bring your date," Kemp chuckled and dug her coffee spoon into her cheesecake.

"Hey! Stop that," she muttered and pulled her plate away.

One thing about her line of work and the people she worked with was that they were all like family. And this was the only family where she felt she belonged. Back at home, with her mom and dad, she felt like the odd one out, simply because she didn't share in their beliefs. She used to, but it all changed in her first year of being a firefighter. It was during that year, where she realized that God helps who he wants to. She had seen too many tragic deaths that included young children and elderly people to think that there was anything merciful about God. After a year of being a firefighter, she eventually opted to take a job in forensics and fire investigations and was transferred. Now instead of running into burning buildings to save people, she now investigated the aftermath instead.

At around noon, after her last case file was concluded, she locked her office and made her way to Franks' to join the others. The atmosphere was festive and the place was crowded. She spotted her colleagues at the far end near the back of the pup and wrangled her way through the crowd.

"Rossouw! You made it, where's Mr. Cheesecake?" Kemp called out raising his beer to her.

She rolled her eyes and laughed, "We had a fight, I left him in the cafeteria to bond with Miss Caramel," she joked.

She ordered herself a cola since she wasn't really one for drinking and joined the rest. The mood was light, and no one spoke about work, which was a relief. She opted for a seat at the far end of the table next to Janet, the receptionist, who was a gray little mouse who barely spoke as it was. She was a bit of an introvert, so other than sipping on her drink she didn't add much value to the conversation. But Christine didn't mind that at all.

It was a while later when a sudden explosion ripped through the kitchen and an orange flame punched its way into the main bar area. Windows shattered and people fell to the ground as smoke and fire billowed into the establishment. Caroline grabbed Jannet and pulled her down to the ground almost instantly as panic erupted. Everywhere people were trying to make it out of the bar, some managing just before the flames engulfed the front entrance.

"Bathroom!" Christine cried out as she tugged Janet's arm, practically dragging her along the side of the wall towards the back where the restrooms were. With any luck they could find a way out through one of the small windows, worst cases they would have water.

The fire alarms erupted over and above the agonizing cries of everyone stuck in the building and Christine knew that if they made it out of here alive, it would be a miracle. Her hope to find an escape route through one of the smaller windows was futile, she might fit through one at a squeeze but Janet won't and she refused to leave the young girl behind. Huddled in the corner of the bathroom, with her arms wrapped around the frantic girl, she could only hope that someone will get to them in time. For the first time in years, she prayed for help.

Christine thought fast, she pulled off her top and drenched it with water, then handed it to Janet, "Here, keep this over your mouth and nose, try to take shallow breaths okay?"

She then grabbed her denim jacket and did the same. Smoke was starting to fill the bathroom and the heat from the main room was slowly pushing towards the back. Time was of the essence, and if the fire department did not arrive soon, they would all meet their maker.

"We're going to die!" Janet panicked.

"No we're not, help is on its way," Christine shouted over the noise of crackling flames and falling banisters.

The sound of approaching sirens was a relief to some extent, at least the fire department was here, but the question that plagued her, was if they would get to them in time. Christine assessed their situation. The fire hadn't reached the restrooms yet, but the heat was excruciating, and smoke pummeled into the small room stealing all the oxygen. She instructed Janet to stay put while she crawled out from under the sink, keeping her body bowed low on the ground. She needed to get to one of the windows and call for help. She felt her way around the floor until she reached one of the cubicles, and then she clambered her way to the window.

"Help! We're in here!" she shouted between bouts of coughs and heaving for air. Her throat was burning and her lungs were filled with smoke, but she refused to give up, "Help!" she called again and again.

"Over here!" she heard someone shout and only then did she allow herself to collapse on the floor. At least now someone would try to get to them.

The last thing she remembered was the incessant smoke that filled the room and the unbearable heat that licked at her skin before her entire world went black.

"Christine! Stay with me!" she recognized the voice from somewhere but she couldn't quite place it, "Christine can you hear me?"

She tried to respond but she simply couldn't. Her brain was doing all the work but the signal to the rest of her body was down. She kept drifting in and out of consciousness but the cool air that surrounded her meant that she was no longer in the inferno. That, or she had died and gone to, wherever bad girls go.

"Where is the ambulance!" she heard her savior call out.

"J... Janet," she managed to utter.

"She's responsive! Christine, it's Jarod, you've had some smoke inhalation, do you know where you are?" she heard him asked.

She tried to open her eyes, but it felt like a million cinders were stuck to her eyeballs, "Where is Janet," she asked first and foremost.

"She's fine, she's alive, thanks to you," he said and squeezed her hand, "But now we need to take care of you."

"Jarod?" she asked half deliriously, "From church?"

He chuckled and brushed her hair from her face, "Yeah Jarod from church, now save your breath. The ambulance will take you to the hospital; I'll come by later to check up on you."

She reached blindly for his hand and squeezed it, "Thank you," she whispered as her head spun and she once again plummeted into a dark hole.

Chapter 4

Jarod was the first to arrive at the hospital, followed by Christine's mom and dad, who both looked like they had been crying.

"Pastor Rossouw..." Jarod started.

"Call me James," he said to Jarod and then introduced his wife, "This is Marjorie, have you heard anything?"

He shook his head, "No I haven't, I'm not family but I know that she had inhaled a lot of smoke, but thankfully the fire never reached them."

"Oh thank you, Lord," her mother exclaimed casting her eyes to the heavens.

"Christine was very brave," Jarod said as he told the couple how she burrowed into the restrooms with her colleague, using very basic methods to keep from suffocating, "When she decided to call for help, was when she inhaled most of the smoke. But if she hadn't done that, no one would have known they were in the bathroom."

Marjorie sat down and cupped her hand over her mouth and James sat down beside her, wrapping his arm around her shoulders, "You were heaven sent," he said to Jarod, "Thank you for saving our little girl."

Jarod smiled and shook his head, "I was just doing my duty sir Pastor."

He left the couple and made his way down the corridor to get some coffee, he was still in uniform, covered in soot and smelling like a furnace, but he didn't want to go until he was a hundred percent sure that Christine was out of danger.

A while later he returned and made his way to where Christine's room was, through the window he saw the Pastor and his wife talking to Christine, who looked like hell but beautiful all the same. She was alive, and by the looks of it, recovering. Thankfully she didn't sustain any burns, it could have been so much worse.

Christine had spotted him just as he was about to leave and waved him over. When he entered the room, her mom and dad excused themselves to go get a bite to eat.

"How are you feeling?" he asked as he pulled a chair closer.

"Like a pizza base right out of the oven?" she said and laughed, but then coughed and clutched her chest, "change that, I feel like I've been to hell and back."

Jarod chuckled and handed her a glass of water, "It was quite something you did back there, your dad mentioned to me you were a firefighter before."

She took a sip of water and counted her breaths, "Yeah, for a year, then I moved to fire forensics."

"I'm glad you didn't forget the training then, it came in handy," he commented.

Even as she lay there, pale as a sheet, with her blond hair still covered in soot and ash, she was beautiful. He never thought that he would even look at another woman after his wife cheated on him, and here he was, doing just that.

He cleared his throat and made an effort to leave, but Christine caught his arm, and smiled, "I owe you dinner and a movie," she said half smiling.

He chuckled and nodded, "As soon as you're back on your feet, I'll come to collect."

Soon he was ushered away when the nurses entered to do the general BP checks, but for a moment he stood looking at her over their heads.

"And the Lord God said, It is not good that a man should be alone," a disembodied voice sounded and Jarod turned to respond, but there was no one else around, other than the nurses going about their business.

Puzzled he turned and looked back at Christine and then waved and left. This was the strangest thing he had ever experienced. It was as if there was someone else there with him, someone far more enlightened than he was. But the words stuck to him all the way home. And he realized beyond a shadow of a doubt that Christine did not appear in his life out of mere coincidence. This was something far bigger than him, or anyone else for that matter.

Chapter 5

Within a few days, Christine was discharged from hospital and sent home to recover. On her mother's insistence, she had no choice but to spend another week staying her folks until she was strong enough to return to work, but every day, Jarod made an effort to visit her, and if he couldn't get to her physically, he would call her. At first, she thought nothing of it, assuming that he was simply being nice, but out of the blue, every time her phone rang and his caller ID flickered on her screen, her stomach would rumble with excitement. Or when she heard his car pull up, she could hardly contain herself. Her dad, of course, wasn't blind either. He knew exactly what was going on.

"Jarod's a fine young man," he said one morning over coffee.

"Yeah, he's nice," she mumbled into her cup.

"Do you like him?"

She whipped her head around and looked at her dad, but the way he smiled at her disarmed her completely and she felt a blush creep into her cheeks, "Yeah, a little."

Her dad chuckled, and Christine put her cup down, "How do you know when you meet the right person?" she asked.

Her dad took his reading glasses off and regarded her, "That's a tough one on answer sweetheart, but sometimes you just know."

She worried her lip and looked into the distance. She had spent all this time guarding her own heart against heartbreak and disappointment. For so long she refused to believe that love existed and convinced herself that she didn't need anyone to go home too. But tragedy has a way to open one's eyes and this is exactly what happened to her. While she was trapped in that restroom practically staring death in the face, her first instinct was to pray and ask God to help her and Janet out of that pickle. It was at that point where she remembered to use what she had to her advantage. And not once during that entire time while they were stuck in that room did she panic, it was an ethereal calm that had taken over and now that she has had time to think it over, she could only come to one conclusion. God had sent His angels to help them. And she was convinced that Jarod was one of them, her personal angel. The thought of him warmed up her heart and a smile spread across her face.

"Penny for your thoughts?" her dad asked.

"I think it's time I go back to church," she said, "and I think I want to give love a chance."

Her dad put his book down and turned to her, smiling, "It's only when you leap into the water that you learn to swim sweetheart. Trust in the Lord and he will make a way clear for you."

Her dad always had wise comebacks, and although she still had a lot to overcome, she knew that little baby steps would eventually get her there.

At around noon, Jared's car rumbled outside, and Christine gave herself one last once-over in the mirror. It was date night, and she was nervous. She tucked a stray strand of hair back into place pulled her lips into a tight pout and released it. It felt as if the muscles in her face were refusing to cooperate.

"Honey!" her mom called and she took a deep steadying breath before making her way to the living room.

When she saw Jared, her heart did that familiar tumble, "Hi," she said and mentally rolled her eyes at her own silliness, "I mean, welcome?" she shook her head, "Never mind, are you ready to go?"

Jared chuckled and nodded at her dad and her mom, "We won't be out very late," he said and Christine literally dragged him out of the house.

"Are you okay?" he asked with a hint of humor in his voice.

"Do I look okay?" she chirped.

"You look fine to me."

Her internal thermometer was about to pop. The way he looked at her when he said she looked fine made her feel all warm and fuzzy inside. She reminded herself that she wasn't a teenager on a first date and forced to compose herself.

"I'm sorry, I just, I haven't been on a date in ages," she said as he opened the passenger door for her.

"Well that makes two of us, so trust me, there's no need to be nervous."

That was a relief she thought, but still, her heart kept thrumming against her chest.

Jarod had surprised her with a visit to a local musical arts theater, where they were hosting a fundraiser for a little girl who needed a skin graph after having sustained serious burns when she was caught in a burning car. Again, he had completely swept her feet out from under her, and she was in complete awe by how passionate he was.

"So do you always get involved in these fundraisers?" she asked curiously over dessert.

He chuckled and reached to wipe a smudge of cream from her chin, "Not always, it depends on the nature of the campaign. Sarah has a special place in my heart, she was only four when the car they were traveling in was involved in a head-on collision. Besides the fact that she was trapped in the burning car, she lost both her parents."

Christine swallowed at the lump in her throat, "That's terrible; I can't even begin to imagine how hard that must be for her."

This was exactly what she couldn't understand, why God would allow such a thing to happen, was just too cruel to comprehend.

"There's actually more to the story than most would believe," he said quietly, "You see, her parents were both alcoholics, and there were a few cases of child abuse against them, but the system failed her. But the funny thing is, after the accident, the driver of the other car, who survived, decided to adopt her and they are paying for all her medical bills."

Christine's jaw dropped and she blinked at the tears that threatened to spill.

"That's nothing short of a miracle," she said softly.

"You can say that again. It's true, God works in mysterious ways, and we don't always know the answers, but He does."

She was both shocked and thrilled by the news, and she couldn't help but cry. Jarod shifted his chair closer to hers and wrapped his arm around her shoulder.

"I didn't mean to make you cry, this is supposed to be the first date," he whispered.

"You didn't make me cry, it's just that," she sniffed against his shoulder, "all this time I figured God was merciless, never once did I consider a bigger picture."

"Shhh," Jarod comforted her and held her close, "It sometimes takes an extraordinary event to make us see things through His eyes, and all I know is that God never fails us, it's only our own expectations."

Chapter 6

Christine took a deep steadying breath as she stood at the end of the aisle, her dad by her side, and Jarod waiting in front, wearing his step out fireman's uniform with all his decorated medals. To the left were all his mates, and the entire squadron of firefighters some wearing their uniforms, other also wearing step outs, to the right was her family and some of her colleagues.

Her big day had arrived; she was finally going to promise herself to the one man she was willing to trust with her life. The wedding march started and she counted her steps in her mind, like a waltz down the aisle.

"I'm so proud to be your father," her dad whispered without moving his lips.

"Daddy you make me proud," she said, "thank you for introducing me to Jared."

Her insides were a kaleidoscope of butterflies and as her father handed her over to her future husband, she couldn't her fingers from trembling, but Jared took her hands in his and smiled at her. His eyes mirrored the same love she felt, and instantly he calmed her down.

It was a day to remember, Christine had not only promised herself to the love of her life, she also found God somewhere in the mix. Somewhere along the line, she realized that God never left; all she had to do was turn around and call on Him.

Christine and Jared lived happily ever after, doing what they both loved and in each other, they found the missing puzzle pieces that made them both complete.

"Are we going to go for green or yellow?" Christine asked holding up two cans of paint.

"Why not do both," Jared said as he worked at assembling the crib.

"Mmm, good point," she said and placed the two small tins on the coffee table, "how is the crib coming along?"

Jared stood up discarding the spanner and pulled his pregnant wife into his arms, "I think we just get our baby to share our bed for a while," he chuckled.

Christine laughed and wrapped her arms around her husband's neck, "I love you," she murmured against his lips.

"And I love you, Christine Marks," Jared said and kissed her.

ANGELA'S CHURCH

Chapter One

Angela packed away the last of her belongings, holding up a crystal vase that had belonged to her mother.

"Please be careful with that," she begged but her words fell on deaf ears as the man roughly grabbed the vase and dumped it into a carton filled with more of Angela's things. She dabbed at her eyes with a wad of tissue and then turned away, unable to bear witness to the horrible sight of her childhood home being robbed of everything that she and her parents had worked so hard to build together.

"Angie, it's your dad," her friend Clara held out her phone.

"Hi Daddy,"Angela said faking a cheerful voice as she took the phone.

She could hear the cough lingering in his voice as he asked her how it was going.

"Oh, it's all good- we're just waiting for them to pack all the boxes into the van. I'll be done here in about half an hour."

There was a brief pause on the other end.

"Half an hour- that's all it'll take to pack up our life in that house. I'll see you soon, darling."

Angela handed the phone back to Clara who shook her head and hugged her.

"It'll be alright, I promise. I'll stay here and get this sorted out, why don't you head over to your new apartment and set it up, hmm?" Clara said affectionately.

Angela nodded, picking up the two boxes which held all the items she had been allowed to keep since they had no resale value. She hailed a cab and read her new address off a scrap of paper. As she sat in the back of the cab with its strange smells and sticky seats, she desperately missed her chauffeur-driven luxury car. She sighed and looked out the window- she could no longer afford to live her old life, and she needed to readjust her standards if she desired any chance of being happy. She was more worried about her father, who had suffered a near-fatal heart attack the moment he had heard the news of his business partner's betrayal.

Decades of hard work, and millions of dollars were lost in the blink of an eye. The bank had seized everything, their house, their things- not even Angela's clothes in her closet were hers anymore; everything belonged to the bank. She was trying to push through it all with a smile on her face, but it was becoming increasingly harder and harder. Her father had been a real-estate mogul for as long as she could remember, and Angela had never wanted for anything growing up. Now, twenty-three years later, here she was, with no money and a very ick father to take care of.

"Here we are," the cab driver called out, and Angela looked up to see the seediest, most damaged building she had ever seen.

"No- that can't be right," she said mostly to herself, but the cabbie shook his head.

"Nope, this is it."

Angela held back her tears and nodded solemnly, rummaging in her wallet for enough money to pay the cab fare.

She carried her boxes over to the shanty building with its peeling paint and overflowing dumpsters, and she whispered a quick prayer, reminding herself that God was just testing her, and that it was all for the better. She took a deep breath and walked inside, where she saw a bored security guard lazily inspecting his nails.

"Excuse me," she said brightly, and the man looked up with an air of apathy.

"Yes?"

Angela set down the boxes and extended her hand but the guard merely looked at it until she withdrew it.

"I'm Angela Wolfe, and I'm renting out apartment 403."

"And?"the guard raised an eyebrow.

"And- hello? Angela licked her lips."That's all I wanted to say really- just introduce myself, that's all."

"Well, you did that."

"Yes- yes I did. Anyway, see you around."

She picked up the boxes and walked towards the elevator when she heard the guard call out.

"It's out of order."

She looked up and saw a notice hanging on the wall, yellowing with age.

"Oh, right. Okay, I'll just take the stairs then."

Once Angela had managed to lug the two boxes up four flights of stairs, she stood outside apartment 403, and took another deep breath.

"Okay," she said to herself, "Moment of truth."

She unlocked the door with the keys she had been given and pushed it open. She was instantly hit with a smell so vile she couldn't describe it, and she covered her nose as she glanced around at the dust-covered rugs and furniture, and the single naked light bulb that hung from the ceiling in the center of what appeared to be the living room. Angela dragged the boxes inside and placed her hands on her hips, resisting the urge to gag from the smell as she looked around.

"Alright- new DIY project. It'll be okay," she said brightly, but her voice cracked at the last word and she knew it wasn't alright- it was far from alright. When she had imagined living in a small rented apartment, she had imagined a cute little terrace where she could place some succulents in cute white planters and a cozy coffee table where she could call her friends and serve them wine and cheese. As she looked around now, she realized she could never invite anybody over. Her old life was gone, and she had to accept it now. She shook her head, and walked out of the apartment, again- it was making her miserable after just five minutes of being in there. She decided to go see her father, even if it meant putting on a performance like she always had to- pretending everything was fine and cheery when they both knew it wasn't.

Chapter Two

She played with her pearls as she sat in the waiting room, the only reminder now of a life she had once led. Her father hadn't let her sell those, and she was glad- they were all she had left of her mother and now they were her only link to the past.

"Miss Wolfe?" The receptionist called out. "Your father's awake- you can go see him now."

Angela looked up, startled out of her thoughts. She thanked the receptionist and made her way to her father's private room- thank goodness for health insurance, or they wouldn't even be able to afford the hospital fees.

"Sweetie," her father said sleepily, "I didn't expect to see you here, weren't you supposed to move into your new place today?"

"Yes, but I missed you too much, so here I am," she said as she gently laid a hand across his forehead.

"Well I'm glad for the company- how's the apartment?"

Her father smiled as he sat up and put on his glasses, For a second, Angela considered breaking down in front of her father but she held it together and smiled.

"Oh, it's just lovely- very cozy and um- quaint."

"Quaint?"her father raised an eyebrow.

"Oh you know, it's very old fashioned- I can spruce it up with a nice rug or two, maybe a lamp," she replied, nodding enthusiastically.

"Angie- if you don't like it, we can set you up somewhere else. What about Clara? I'm sure you can spend some time with her."

"No, no it's a lovely place, don't worry. And I wouldn't want to burden Clara anyway, she's getting married in two months and I would just be in the way,"she said.

"Daddy- please you have to rest!"Angela said hurrying over to him as he tried to get up but he grimaced with pain and fell back into bed.

"Fetch me that file, would you?" he nodded and pointed to a table in the corner

"What's that?"

Angela picked up the clear folder and handed it to him.

"It just might be our salvation." He pulled out a sheaf of paper.

"Yes- just as I had hoped, it's not in the company's name."

"What's not in the company's name?" she inquired curiously – craning her neck trying to glance at the paper but it was too far away.

"Angie, there's an old property on the edge of town- I acquired it very early on, before we established Wolfe-Moore Industries, and if we restore it and sell it, we can earn a pretty good sum from it," he said gravely as he sat up again and took off his glasses. He handed her the document.

"But it has to be you- only you can handle the property."

As Angela pored over the sheet, she realized why it had to be her- the name on the deed was her mother's, and according to her mother's will, Angela had inherited all her property.

"So this property- it belongs to me?" She asked uncertainly and her father nodded.

"Daddy, it's too much. We've lost everything, can't you see that? This one little house isn't going to change anything, no matter who buys it, and why would anyone purchase anything from us anyway? We're bankrupt, the whole company's been exposed in all of the newspapers; everyone knows we haven't got two cents to rub together. I walked here, Daddy, because I didn't have enough to pay the cab driver- can you believe that? I walked here my horrible rat-infested building to this hospital which is like ten blocks, but I didn't have a choice because we're poor," she said in an unexpected fit of rage.

After she was done, she held onto the bedpost to stop herself from swaying.

"I'm sorry," she said meekly. But to her surprise, her father laughed.

"You look just like your mother when you get angry- she also yelled at me like that quite often."

Angela crossed her arms over her chest, and smiled reluctantly.

"So I was right- you don't like your apartment?" he added.

Angela shrugged and said,

"No- it's alright. I mean- yeah I hate it. It's terrible, Daddy- it smells so bad and I think there might be a small animal living in there," she said shrugging her shoulders.

He laughed again and she smiled, it was good to hear him laugh after all this time.

"That's why I'm so keen on restoring this property, Angie. It's a good one I promise, and once you work your magic on it, it will make things a lot easier for us."

"You're not gonna let this go, are you? Always a businessman- even from the hospital bed," she shook her head and sighed.

"So you'll do it?"

"Yes, I'll do it- like I could have ever said no to you anyway. So what is this property anyway?"

"It's beautiful, Angela, it's just a stunning structure- The Trinity Church," he answered beaming widely.

Chapter Three

Angela climbed out of the car and gazed up in awe of the beautiful structure. It was a huge gothic church, complete with its pointed arches and ribbed vaults. Clara climbed out beside her and stood with her as the two gazed on silently, stunned speechless by the church's majesty. As they looked on, however, they realized the church was actually falling apart.

The flying buttresses were crumbling, threatening to collapse any second, and Angela instinctively knew that her father was right- saving this church meant saving their family. Clara patted her gently on the shoulder and Angela smiled.

"Shall we go inside?" Angela asked Clara.

"Oh please- let's."

The two women took deep breaths and walked purposefully towards the giant doors of the church. They were heavy and needed their combined strength to push them open. Clara immediately started coughing as the dust swirled inside and Angela looked around, fascinated but dismayed at the amount of work that would be needed.

She was unusually quiet on the drive back, and listened silently as Clara went on and on, about the church and the country club and her fiancé.

"Angie!"

"Sorry- I was thinking about the church. Clara, I'll need to hire someone; a contactor. But I don't have any money," she was startled out of her thoughts.

Clara frowned as she thought about it.

"Oh I know! You know David volunteers at our church whenever he can-" she said brightly as she got a brainwave.

"Oh God, Clara- can you stop talking about your fiancé and help me out?"

Clara shot Angela a withering look and continued on.

"As I was saying, *David* works with some men who are recovering addicts trying to find their way back to God, and they're being given some vocational training. I'll ask him if there are any construction workers or contractors he could send your way. They charge very little, so it shouldn't be a problem."

Angela suddenly felt terrible about snapping at her best friend, but before she could even apologize, Clara waved a hand dismissively.

"Don't worry about it. I know you're stressed. Okay, so where should I drop you, the hospital or your apartment?"

"The hospital please," Angela said quickly, not wanting to show Clara where she lived just yet.

As they pulled up to the hospital, Angela thanked Clara and quickly hurried off, so her friend wouldn't ask her too many questions or guess that she was trying to hide something.

She walked quickly to her father's room but slowed down as she neared the door to his ward. She often had to prepare herself before she walked in- it was always so hard to see her father like that. Angela's mother had passed away when she was ten years old, and for the next fourteen years, she had seen her father as her pillar of strength. Too see him lying in a hospital bed connected to tubes and machines was always very difficult for her.

"Hi Daddy," she called out when she walked in. He lowered the book he was reading and smiled.

"Hi sweetheart, I didn't expect to see you today. Weren't you going to go see the church?"

"Mmhmm, I did go. It's a beautiful old church, but it's a lot of work," she said nodding and peering at the book cover.

Her father tried to sit up but Angela looked at him sternly and he lay back down with a sigh.

"I know, I know- it's crumbling but it would be such a shame to let it go to waste. Come on, tell me what you really thought."

"It really is gorgeous- and the architecture is just exquisite. I mean the arches, and I think I saw the remains of a stained-glass window. Truly stunning, I can see why you held onto it for so long," she accepted with a smile.

Her father didn't say anything, but when Angela looked at him, he had tears in his eyes.

"Dad, what's wrong?"

"Your mother loved that old church. She was always telling me to work on it but I was so busy with other things, things I thought more profitable-"

"Maybe this was fate. Maybe it was meant to be this way- that I would restore it for her."

Her father held her hand to his heart and then wept softly, and Angela tried very hard to fight back her own tears, but in vain.

When the nurse walked in a minute later, she was startled and ashamed of intruding on them.

"I'll come back later," she mumbled and left.

"No- please, you go ahead. I have to run anyway," she kissed the top of her father's balding head and said, "Bye Daddy."

She hurried out of the room before he could say anything and when she was outside, she leaned against the wall for a few minutes trying to put herself together again. Somehow, speaking about her mother always made her emotional, even after all this time had passed. Being in the hospital reminded her of the time when her mother was sick and it brought back the terrible feeling of loss and the fear of losing a parent.

Once she had managed to collect herself, she walked out of the hospital and got a cab to take her to the new apartment. As she walked up the dirty stairwell, she felt like breaking down- everything in her life was so overwhelmingly difficult all at once and she didn't know if she would be able to make it. For the first time in a long time, she stopped where she was and pressed her palms together as she began to pray.

A few people passed her by on the stairs, but Angela continued to pray until she felt better, and then she slowly continued up the stairs, reaching her apartment and taking a deep breath. "I can do this," she said to herself, and pushed the door open.

The same dust and smell rose to greet her, but this time, she was determined to stop feeling miserable and do something about it. She walked straight towards the kitchen and picked up the cleaning supplies she had bought earlier that day.

"Alright," she said looking around, not knowing where to start, "Let's clean this mess."

Chapter Four

Angela had started to pick her way through the dusty pews when she heard the car pull up. Excitedly, she turned back and walked to the large double doors. As she neared the entrance, a tall man walked through- he was lanky and thin and had the air of someone who had lost a lot of weight all at once and far too quickly. He smiled pleasantly and held his hand out.

"Hello- you must be Angela. I'm Nathan, nice to meet you."

Angela shook his hand and greeted him warmly, showing him into the church as though she were welcoming a guest into her home.

"So this place really is something, huh?" he said looking around – letting out a low whistle.

"Nothing a little bit of love and care won't fix," she said confidently.

"No, I mean look at it- it's beautiful."

Angela was surprised to see someone like him stand so in awe of a church and she quickly reminded herself not to judge a book by its cover- even of the cover looked shabby and dog-eared.

That's what Nathan looked like- as though he was worn out with time and usage, his young body ageing rapidly as his muscles atrophied. There was a slight revulsion that Angela felt and she tried very hard to control it as she showed him around. He seemed enthusiastic about the work though and Angela was glad about that.

"You know, that window could be re-painted, the pews can be polished, and I can take a look at the buttressed right away, they seem to be weakening with age." He was talking fast and Angela nodded quickly, feeling much more reassured about him and his abilities.

"Excellent, yes we can start right away if you like. I'll have a contract drawn up tomorrow so that we discuss your salary-" but he didn't let her finish as he waved a hand dismissively.

"No no, I'm just looking for work, but I don't need to be paid. Especially for a project like this- it's so meaningful."

Angela bristled for a moment as she thought that Clara might have told David why this church was so important to Angela, and David might have told Nathan, but then she quickly realized that Nathan had simply meant that it was meaningful because it was a church. She also remembered what Clara had told her about Nathan trying to find his way back to God.

"Are you sure you don't want me to pay you? I mean you can't work for free."

"No, for this kind of project I could enter ask for payment. This is God's work, and if I'm successful I will owe it all to you and to Him," he said shaking his head.

Angela stood in awe of him and suddenly felt terrible for thinking the worst of him when she first saw him.

"I- This church means a lot to me," Angela said, and she expected him to ask her why.

"Well then I want to make sure that I do a good job," he replied acting indifferent to its backstory.

Angela watched him as he walked around the church, inspecting things and talking to himself, she felt a strange feeling that she could not describe. She shook her head and focused on the task ahead, ignoring the sensation in her belly and joining Nathan in examining the walls and frescoes.

"This is gorgeous work- but I'm worried there might be mold lurking around somewhere. It's a difficult job for sure- do you mind if I bring a team of my men with me to help out?"

Angela blinked- the thought of having strange men surround her in an abandoned church should have caused her to panic, but instead she found herself nodding.

"Yeah- that's great, we should be done sooner then."

Nathan smiled and continued, and even though Angela followed him, she wasn't listening to what he was saying. Instead, she looked at him- really looked. He had a tall, thin frame but he was surprisingly strong and could lift things out of the way very easily, his clothes were old but neatly pressed and mended in some places, and they were far too big for him. He had light brown hair that was swept back from his face and green eyes that were so large they looked almost out of place on his thin face.

At one point, Nathan saw him looking at her and smiled, catching Angela off guard. She turned red and fluttered her eyelashes embarrassedly, quickly pretending to be looking at the stained glass work on the windows instead, and letting her long black hair fall forwards to cover her face.

She was trying to be quiet as a mouse so she wouldn't draw attention to herself just now, and suddenly, her phone started to ring. She leapt up, startled, and pulled her phone out of her pocket.

"Hey Clara," she said into the phone with a sigh.

"Angie- how's everything? Did the contractor get there?"

Angela dropped her voice and edged towards the door.

"Yes, he's here. He seems like he knows what he's doing, so tell David thanks please," she whispered into the phone.

"It's Nathan right? He's really wonderful, and he's very hard-working, but if he gives you any trouble, just tell David, okay?"

Angle thanked her friend and hung up, turning around and gasping when she found Nathan inches away from her.

"Sorry, I didn't mean to creep up on you," he said, blinking at her with those strange green eyes of his, "But I'm done with the notes and calculations. I can go back and get the materials now- would you like me to drop you home on the way?"

Angela nodded, not wishing to be stranded out here trying to catch a cab, but still not comfortable with letting people know where she lived. She glanced at him as they walked out of the church, and wondered where he lived- would he judge her building and apartment if he saw it? Did he live in worse conditions? She shook her head slightly, feeling terrible for assuming that he lived in poverty.

She climbed into the passenger seat and looked out of the window, smiling slightly at Nathan as he climbed in from the other side and revved the engine.

Chapter Five

As they neared her building, Angela considered asking him to drop her off somewhere else like a supermarket, but she stayed quiet and let him drive on.

"It's the next left, right?" Nathan asked when they were almost there.

Angela nodded, waiting for it to be over.

"Here we are," he said as he pulled up and passed her a smile.

She suddenly felt a lot more at ease- he hadn't reacted at all.

"Would you like to come upstairs? I can make some coffee," she asked spontaneously.

Nathan's expression changed to one of wonder, and Angela worried that she may have made a mistake.

"I'd love to. I haven't had a good cup of coffee in days," he replied cheerfully.

Angela led him upstairs and he followed quietly until they reached her apartment. She considered warning him that it wasn't entirely clean yet, but she didn't. Instead, she pushed open the door and welcomed him in. He smiled as he stepped inside; looking around as he nervously wrung his hands together. Angela looked around too- she had cleaned up a little bit, and the dust was all gone, replaced by some rugs from the old house and two small armchairs. She had put small planters on the windowsill to hide the ugly view of the neighbor's clotheslines. She anxiously waited for Nathan to say something, but he didn't, and she was glad.

"Why don't you take a seat," she said gesturing to the armchairs, "And I'll make us some coffee?"

Nathan hesitantly sat down, still fidgeting nervously, and Angela went off to the kitchen, pulling out mugs as she thought about the fact that there was a strange man in her house. She had only known Nathan for a few hours but somehow, she felt comfortable enough around him to know that she needn't worry. She heaped a spoonful or two of coffee powder into mugs and added sugar and cream, before carrying it out in a small tray.

"Sorry, I only have instant coffee- I hope that's alright," she said, setting the tray down and handing him a mug.

"No, that's perfect- thank you," he said taking the warm mug in both hands.

She was settling into the other armchair when her phone began to ring.

"Sorry," she muttered fishing it out her pocket and answering it.

"Miss Wolfe?" A voice urgently said on the other line, "It's Nurse Farris from the hospital- I'm afraid your father's had another heart attack. The doctors are seeing to him now and he's under care but I suggest you come down here quickly."

Angela nearly dropped the phone and without a word she turned and ran to the door.

"Miss Wolfe?" Nathan called out, "Miss Wolfe?" He started to follow her out the door, pulling it shut behind him. She ran down the stairs not answering him, and he caught up with her, "What's wrong? Do you need to go somewhere? I can drive you."

Angela turned to him, ashen-faced as she nodded.

"Hospital," was the only word she could manage to utter.

Nathan didn't say another word, he led her to the car and unlocked the passenger door for her, hurrying over to the other side and climbing in. They drove quietly for a few minutes until Nathan broke the silence.

"Madison Memorial?"

Angela nodded and looked out of window wordlessly.

"Miss Wolfe, is there something I can do?" He asked, after some time, glancing sideways at her as they stopped at a red light.

"Angela," she said quietly. He looked at her, confused, and she said, "Call me Angela, please."

"Um- Angela," he gulped as he spoke."What happened? Why are we going to the hospital? I mean unless you don't want to tell me- that's alright too and-"

"It's my father." She spoke so quietly that Nathan had to make sure he hadn't misheard her.

"You father? Is he alright?"

Angela shook her head and Nathan mentally chided himself- of course her father wasn't alright, that's why he was in the hospital. He glanced again at the beautiful woman sitting next to him, and he wondered about her. He had assumed she was wealthy by the pearls around her neck and her general air, but then he had seen her apartment and reconsidered his first judgment. Now, he was itching to know more about this mysterious woman and the strange double life she seemed to lead. He was panicking because he felt that he ought to do something to help her, but he didn't know what.

"Angela?" He said after some time, as they were pulling into the hospital's driveway. "We're here."

"Right. Well, thank you," she said absent mindedly as she sat up as though he had woken her from a dream.She pushed open the car door and left without even closing it. Nathan leaned toward and pulled it shut and then parked the car before he got out. Angela had disappeared but he walked into the building and headed for the reception desk.An impatient woman glared at him.and he said,

"Um- I'm here to see Mr. Wolfe?" he said.

She scanned the list in front of her and told him a room number. He headed for the elevator and wondered whether he should be going up there.

Something kept him going, and even though he considered turning back several ties, a few minutes later he found himself standing outside a door which had "Wolfe" scrawled next to it in black marker. Taking a deep breath and squaring his shoulders, Nathan knocked on the door and waited for what seemed like an eternity for it to open. Finally, he heard footsteps approaching and he held his breath- the door was pulled open and there stood Angela with her black hair streaming down her back and shoulders, and tears clinging to her eyelashes. She blinked at him for a second, her face completely blank, and then suddenly, she threw her arms around his neck and sobbed onto his shoulder.

Chapter Six

They sat cross-legged on the rooftop of the hospital, and Angela rubbed her arms to protect herself from the chilly night air.

"Here," Nathan said, draping his jacket over her shoulders.

"No, you really don't have to-" Angela protested but Nathan shook his head and sat down.

"Thank you- for staying I mean. Daddy's surgery will take so long, and I really didn't want to be alone. But I don't know who else I could be with right now."

"It's no problem at all. I'm happy to be here," he cleared his throat and said, "If you don't mind me asking, how long has he been sick?"

Angela sighed and looked away, taking in the view from the rooftop- the stars seemed closer here, and they blinked brightly, fighting through the light pollution to shine down on her.

"If you don't want to tell me, that's alright, I respect that," Nathan said, smiling in such an easygoing manner that for a moment, Angela almost forgot her troubles, before they came crashing back and she shook her head.

"It's not that- I just don't know where to start. Well, I guess I do." She sighed and went on, "My father spent his life building an empire- he put his life and soul into his real estate business and it grew. I remember living comfortably when I was little, but as I grew up, so did our wealth. A few months ago, we were living so fabulously, it was almost sinful. But it all came to an end."

Nathan edged forward, furrowing his brows with concern.

"My father's best friend was always interested in the business, and he always said he wanted to learn so my father let him join. He made a few investments and came on the executive board. It was soon after that the accounts stopped adding up- we were losing money and nobody knew where it was going. Well, we eventually figured it out- Daddy's best friend was embezzling. But he had powerful contacts and he got out while the business crashed to the ground. The bank seized our house, and we lost everything. My father had a heart attack when he discovered that his best friend had betrayed him."

"Wow- I can't believe people do these things to their loved ones," he muttered while shaking his head.

"Well, there are some horrible people in the world. Snakes that pretend to care about you and then leave you with nothing- my father is a good person. He didn't deserve this, nobody does."

"I think you're a good person too, and I think that your father is very proud of the work that you're doing," he said nearing in.

Angela glanced up, startled.

"I know why you're so interested in restoring in that church. It's a way to salvage your father's work, and give him some peace of mind, isn't it?"

Angela nodded, and she moved closer to Nathan as well, aware of his knees touching hers now.

"I think you're a very good person, Angela."

"I think you are too- Clara told me about the program, and how it's helping you. That's admirable," she said with a warm smile.

"Maybe we can help each other," he said as he reached out to take hold of her hand.

Angela glanced at their intertwined fingers and then at him as she nodded.

"Maybe we can," before she leaned forward and gently pressed her lips against his.

They stayed like that, their cross-legged figures lit by the gentle moonlight, brought together by fate but both seeking salvation and maybe finding it in each other.

www.ingramcontent.com/pod-product-compliance
Lightning Source LLC
Chambersburg PA
CBHW022138150726
47992CB00002B/661